NANEA
1941

Hula for the Home Front

by Kirby Larson

★ American Girl®

Honolulu, Hawaii

It's 1942, and everyone in Hawaii
is doing their part to help the
war effort. Nanea is happy
when her 'ohana–her family–
comes together to create special
memories at the beach.

18 EXPOSURES
FILM

18 EXPOSU
FILM

TARGET
BROWNIE SIX-20

April 11, 1942

Nanea's Family and Friends

Papa & Mom
Nanea's parents

David
Nanea's 17-year-old brother

Mary Lou
Nanea's 15-year-old sister

Tutu & Tutu Kane
Nanea's grandparents

Auntie Rose
*Nanea's next-door neighbor,
who makes flower leis*

Lily
Nanea's oldest friend

Tommy
*Lily's younger brother,
who is 5*

Gene
Lily's older brother, who is 17

Aunt Betty & Uncle Fudge
Lily's parents

Dixie
*A girl in Nanea's class who has
just moved to Honolulu*

Mrs. Lin
*A neighbor of Nanea's
who owns a small shop*

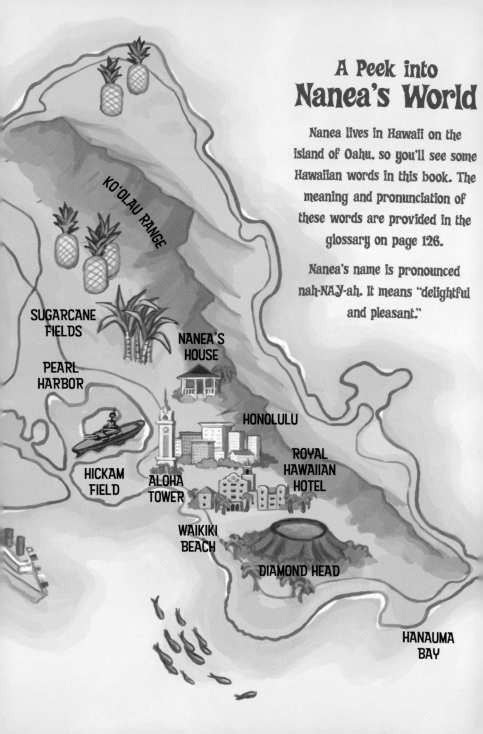

A Peek into Nanea's World

Nanea lives in Hawaii on the island of Oahu, so you'll see some Hawaiian words in this book. The meaning and pronunciation of these words are provided in the glossary on page 126.

Nanea's name is pronounced nah-NAY-ah. It means "delightful and pleasant."

KO'OLAU RANGE

SUGARCANE FIELDS

NANEA'S HOUSE

PEARL HARBOR

HONOLULU

ROYAL HAWAIIAN HOTEL

HICKAM FIELD

ALOHA TOWER

WAIKIKI BEACH

DIAMOND HEAD

HANAUMA BAY

Table of Contents

A Lauhala Family

Nanea Mitchell lay in bed, pretending to sleep, while her big sister, Mary Lou, got ready. School was finally in session again after the Pearl Harbor attacks, and Mary Lou was going early to hang up "Welcome Back" banners at McKinley High.

After she finished her hair, Mary Lou grabbed the knitting bag she carried everywhere these days. She tiptoed out of their shared room as if she thought Nanea was asleep.

Nanea shifted, hugging her knees to her chest. She'd hardly slept the night before. It was finally February second, and until a few days ago, she had been so eager for this morning to come. Going back to school meant forgetting about blackouts and curfews and air-raid drills. Sitting in Miss Smith's classroom at Lunalilo Elementary, Nanea would be surrounded by friends and would get lost in spelling bees and flash cards and her teacher's lively stories. It was going to be wonderful.

But then everything changed. The Three Kittens— Nanea and her two best friends, Lily Suda and Donna Hill—were split apart. The military government had been in charge since the attack on Pearl Harbor, and it decided people like Donna and her mom were "nonessential civilians." They weren't directly helping the war effort, so they had to leave the island. Last Friday, Nanea and Lily had gone to the pier to say a final good-bye to Donna and her mother before they sailed off to San Francisco.

Nanea sighed heavily. Her dog, *Mele*, who had been sleeping on the floor next to her bed, stood on her hind legs to peer over the edge of the mattress. Nanea pulled back her quilt and patted the bed. Mele hopped up and snuggled against Nanea's side.

Nanea held her close, breathing in her doggy smell. Mele had gone missing after the attacks, and for two long weeks, Nanea had searched high and low for her. Since they'd been reunited, Mele didn't like to let Nanea out of her sight. That was just fine with Nanea.

"I couldn't stand to lose you again," Nanea said, giving the dog a squeeze as she remembered that awful time.

Mele shifted, and a newspaper clipping fell from the nightstand onto the bed. It was from yesterday's paper.

Nanea picked it up and studied the picture of herself with Lily and Donna and a group of their friends. Her family was so proud of Nanea for organizing a bottle drive for the Red Cross. The girls had collected over a thousand bottles so far. They'd had their picture taken for the newspaper, and Nanea had even been interviewed by Miss Gwenfread Allen, a real reporter.

Nanea had smiled big for the newspaper photo, which had been taken the day before Donna left. Now when she looked at the picture, Nanea couldn't think about the bottle drive. She could only think of how much she missed Donna. Mele thumped her tail on the bed.

"Okay, I'll read it to you again," Nanea said.

I recently had the pleasure of conversing with Miss Alice Nanea Mitchell—who goes by her Hawaiian name, Nanea—a poised and thoughtful young lady. Though Nanea was shy about taking credit, her friends assured me that she was the brains behind the highly successful bottle drive to benefit the Red Cross blood center. She says she was inspired by her brother's work in the hospital in the days after the attacks, when he delivered bottles of blood to those in critical need. When she learned that Honolulu was long on blood donors but short on bottles, Nanea sprang to action.

Despite her accomplishments, this young lady confesses to losing sleep most nights. Each time she heads to her family's air-raid shelter, she wonders if it's the real McCoy. She and her

*friends long for the return of their carefree island days. Days
filled with jacks and jump rope and bike rides to the beach. Days
where one's biggest concern was what flavor shave ice to order.
While the war has required that we all make sacrifices, those
paying the dearest price are our children.*

Miss Allen's last words reminded Nanea again of how
much she had given up, including one of her best friends.
How could she go to school without Donna? She wished
Papa were home so she could talk to him. He always made
her feel better. But he was working another double shift at
the Pearl Harbor shipyard.

Mele licked Nanea's face.

"I know. It's time to get up." Nanea placed the newspaper clipping back on her nightstand and dragged herself
out of bed. She pulled on a school dress. It was red with
blue trim. Blue was Donna's favorite color. Nanea sat back
down on her bed, thinking about Donna.

Nanea's seventeen-year-old brother, David, stuck his
head through the doorway. "Breakfast is about ready," he
announced. Then he looked at Nanea's face. "What's up,
Monkey?" he asked.

"I don't know," Nanea answered, even though she did
know. She was afraid if she told David, she'd start crying.
And if she started, she might not stop!

David stepped into the room. "Shove over," he said.

Nanea made room for him on the edge of the mattress.

"You don't have to tell me," he said. "But does it have something to do with that?" He pointed at the article.

"I know it's an honor to be in the paper," Nanea started. Papa was so proud that he'd sent a copy of the article to Nanea's grandparents in Oregon.

"But?" David prompted.

"But it's like Miss Allen said. Too many things have changed." Nanea thought about how her island life used to be full of picnics at the beach, fishing with Papa, and playing outside in the long evening shadows. Now there was war. She couldn't stop the tear that trickled down her cheek. "The beaches are blocked by barbed wire. Papa's working all the time so we never go fishing anymore. We all have to sit in the dark night after night during the blackouts. One of my best friends is gone, and the other one . . ." Nanea's voice trailed off.

"What?" David asked.

Nanea leaned against David's strong shoulder, breathing in his familiar smell of Old Spice. "Lily and I were walking home from Mrs. Lin's crack seed shop yesterday when someone yelled something not very nice at Lily—"

"—because she's Japanese." David finished Nanea's sentence for her.

Nanea nodded. "There are too many problems. And all of them are too big."

David's shirt was damp with Nanea's tears. "Monkey, I wish I could say that everything will get better soon. But nobody knows when this war will end." He tapped her gently on the arm. "There is one thing I can tell you for sure."

Nanea tipped her head up to look into David's face. "What?" she asked, doubtfully. Her brother's Hawaiian name was Kekoa, which meant brave and strong. But not even David was strong enough to make the war stop.

"You don't have to face this alone. Your *'ohana*, your family, is here with you," he said. Then he picked up the small *lauhala* basket full of barrettes that Nanea kept on the dresser. "Think about this basket. One *hala* leaf is woven with another and another. Together, the leaves create something strong and sturdy. Just like our *'ohana*."

Nanea reached for the basket and turned it around in her hands, thinking about how her mom and dad, brother and sister, and grandparents were part of the weaving of her life.

"We all have to work together to win this war." David stood up. "The more everyone helps, the sooner things can get back to normal. I can tell you one more thing for certain."

Nanea returned the basket to the dresser. "What?"

"Mom is going to fuss if we aren't at the breakfast table right away." He smiled his movie-star smile at her, tapping the door frame as he left the room.

Nanea clipped a barrette in her hair. "I guess I could manage a little something for breakfast," she said to Mele. "And I know *you* can always eat." She picked up her dog and cuddled her close. Nanea tried not to miss Donna, but it was impossible. Her friend was as much a part of the weaving of her life as Mele was.

Right-Hand Girl
CHAPTER 2

anea had just finished brushing her teeth when Lily knocked at the front door. "Are you ready?" Lily called.

"Yes." Nanea swung her gas-mask bag over one shoulder and her book bag over the other. Inside the book bag was a woven bookmark that Nanea had made for Miss Smith. Miss Smith always called Nanea her "right-hand girl," so Nanea had taken care to make her teacher a special welcome-back present.

Mom kissed the top of Nanea's head. "Do your best today," she said.

With Mele trotting behind, the girls walked down Fern Street. When they turned onto Pumehana Avenue, Nanea couldn't keep from looking over at Donna's house. She so wished there was a blonde-haired girl on the front steps, chewing a piece of Bazooka bubble gum, waiting to walk to school with them.

Lily looked, too. "I miss Donna," she said, shifting her gas-mask strap to the other shoulder with a sigh.

"I'm going to write her as soon as I get home from

school today," Nanea said. "I'll tell her everything that happened."

"Great idea!" Lily stepped over a gecko that was sunning itself on the sidewalk. "I will, too."

Across the street from the school, Nanea stopped to say good-bye to Mele. "See you this afternoon, girl." Nanea knelt down to give Mele a hug, but as she tried to stand, the weight of the gas mask and the book bag pulled her right over. She was flat on her back.

"Help!" Nanea flailed her arms.

"You look like a pill bug," Lily said, reaching out a hand to help. She began to giggle.

"I feel like one!" Nanea got to her feet, laughing as well. It felt good to laugh. "Did I get any dirt on my dress?" She turned around and Lily patted at the skirt.

"Good as new," Lily pronounced.

"I hope so." Nanea grinned. "It *is* new!" Nanea turned to Mele. "Now, you head on home."

Mele hesitated. This would be the first time they'd been apart all day since Nanea found Mele after the bombing.

"It'll be okay," Nanea said gently. "I'll be home before you know it."

Reluctantly, Mele trotted off, and the girls crossed the street. Normally, Nanea and Lily would've climbed the worn wooden stairs to their classroom on the second

floor. But the stairs were now blocked by ropes that were tied between the bannisters. Up above, workers were still repairing the library and classrooms that had been damaged by the fire on December seventh. That was one more thing that had changed because of the war.

The girls made their way to a smaller room on the first floor and squeezed through the aisles. They took the same seats near the window that they'd had in their old classroom and hung their gas masks on the backs of their chairs. Miss Smith wasn't there yet, so Nanea hurried to place the neatly wrapped bookmark on her teacher's desk. On her way back to her seat, she smiled to think how surprised Miss Smith would be and how much she'd like the present. She'd probably use it right away!

More kids wandered in, including a girl Nanea hadn't seen before. Finally, Miss Smith sailed into the classroom. "Good morning, scholars," she said.

"Good morning, Miss Smith," Nanea and her classmates answered.

"Oh my goodness!" Miss Smith pressed her hands to her cheeks. "To see your smiling faces is a dream come true."

The cares and worries of the past months slipped off Nanea's shoulders. Miss Smith was like Superman, swooping in to save them all from the troubles of the world. Miss Smith asked Lily to lead the flag salute. Then she took attendance. The new girl answered, "here," when Miss Smith called out, "Dixie Moreno."

"Dixie, we're so glad you've joined our class," Miss Smith said. "Would you like to tell us a bit about yourself?"

Dixie wore a short brown pageboy haircut and a slightly crooked smile. She stood up confidently at her desk. "I've moved here from Maui because my dad has a new job at Wheeler Airfield. We're living with my aunt and uncle for now. I love tap dancing, and when I'm older I'm getting three dogs." She smiled. "I can't have pets now because my aunt's allergic." She sat down.

"Thank you, Dixie," Miss Smith said. "Welcome to

Lunalilo. I think you'll find we're a friendly crew."

Nanea didn't feel completely friendly toward Dixie, who was sitting where Donna should be. But Nanea did feel bad that Dixie wanted a dog and couldn't have one. She gave her a smile, and Dixie smiled back, but the smile turned into a yawn, which Dixie covered with her hand.

"Now, before we begin our lessons, I have an exciting opportunity to tell you about," Miss Smith announced. "We'll be having a weekly War Stamp sale in the classroom. Every stamp helps the war effort, so please pitch in as much as you can." Then Miss Smith cleared her throat. "If ninety percent of the class buys stamps, we can earn a Minuteman flag." She clasped her hands together. "Just imagine that special flag flying over our school, showing Honolulu, Oahu—the world—that we are doing our part here at Lunalilo to help the war effort!"

The class murmured with excitement. "I've seen a real Minuteman flag," Albert Ogawa announced. "They're nifty."

Miss Smith's eyes sparkled and her cheeks turned rosy with excitement. "I know many of you have uncles and brothers and fathers who are serving in the military. My own brother is in the Army Air Forces. I wonder if you scholars would like to dedicate our stamp drive to those brave men." She took a picture frame from her desk and turned it around so the class could see her brother's photo. He was dressed in uniform and smiled proudly.

Nanea glanced around the room. She could tell from her schoolmates' faces that they all felt as she did. They would not let Miss Smith, or her brother, or any of their family members, down. They would do their part for the war effort and earn a Minuteman flag!

When the lunch bell rang, Lily grabbed her paper sack and her jacks set. "Should we ask the new girl to join us?"

Nanea didn't really want to invite Dixie, but her mother had taught her to always be welcoming to someone new. She glanced over at Dixie, who had pulled a book out of her bag and was unwrapping a sandwich at her desk. "It looks like she's staying in," Nanea said.

"Oh, okay." Lily followed Nanea out of the room.

Outside, Nanea reached into her lunch pail. Mom had made her a bologna sandwich. Donna's favorite. But there wouldn't be any trading today because Donna wasn't there. "What do you think Donna's getting for lunch on the ship?" Nanea asked. "Do you think it's something special for their last day at sea?"

Lily put a straw in her milk bottle. "I bet she gets chocolate cake for dessert." That was Lily's favorite.

"With ice cream!" Nanea added. She imagined Donna and her mother all dressed up in the ship's elegant dining room, curling their pinkies as they sipped tea from delicate china cups. Someday Nanea would take a trip on a Matson liner and dine on fancy meals with rich desserts. Until then, she'd be happy with Mom's homemade peanut butter cookies.

When she and Lily went back to class after lunch, Dixie was still at her desk, but now Miss Smith was sitting next to her. Dixie was showing their teacher something in the book she was reading. Dixie and Miss Smith both laughed.

The bologna sandwich turned to lead in Nanea's stomach. Miss Smith was acting like *Dixie* was her right-hand girl! Nanea felt a little crab-pinch of jealousy.

Miss Smith kept the class hopping the rest of the afternoon. She gave them a math pop quiz, and then they had a boys-against-girls spelling relay. Nanea's word was "dream," which she quickly spelled correctly. She ran back to her desk to tag Dixie. Dixie's word was "sitting," but she left out the second *t* so the girls lost the relay. Dixie didn't even say she was sorry. She just yawned like she was bored with it all.

When the bell rang at the end of the day, the students

jumped up to gather their belongings.

"Oh, Nanea," Miss Smith called. "Would you mind staying after a moment?"

Nanea smiled. "Wait for me," she said to Lily.

Lily nodded. "I'll be out front."

Nanea approached the teacher's desk expectantly.

"Thank you so much for this beautiful gift." Miss Smith held up a book with Nanea's bookmark peeking out. "I've already put it to good use."

"I thought you would like it," Nanea said, pleased that she knew her teacher so well.

Miss Smith leaned toward Nanea, as if sharing a secret. "You are my right-hand girl," she said. "So I have a very important job for you."

"I can do it!" Nanea said confidently.

Miss Smith fiddled with her earring. "Dixie was feeling a little sad today so I let her stay inside for lunch. But I know she'd have more fun playing outside. I'd like you to be her special buddy. Help her get to know her classmates. Make her feel welcome."

"Dixie?" Nanea blinked. Miss Smith wanted Nanea to buddy up to a bad speller!

"Thank you, dear." Miss Smith pushed her chair back from her desk. "I knew I could count on you."

Poster Problems

On Friday morning, Nanea folded her letter to Donna and slid it into an envelope. Then she picked up the three-cent stamp Mom had given her. "This is the second letter I've written to Donna since she left," Nanea said. She licked the stamp and pasted it to the envelope. "I wonder why I haven't gotten one from her yet."

Mom wrapped Nanea's peanut butter sandwich in wax paper. "Be patient, honey. Donna only left a week ago. And things are slow at the post office because the mail is being censored." Mom tucked the sandwich into Nanea's blue lunch pail. "Every letter going out and coming in has to be read by an official before it's delivered."

Mary Lou squeezed lemon juice over her papaya. "And there are all kinds of rules about what you can put in a letter."

"You can't even write about the weather," David added. "If the enemy got ahold of the mail, that information could help them plan an attack." He stood up and cleared his breakfast dishes. "I'm heading out. I'll be home late because of that training for my new job."

Nanea took a bite of toast. "Isn't working at the hotel enough?" David already had a job at the Royal Hawaiian.

"There's not much of a need for bellboys these days," he answered.

Nanea sighed. Because of the war, the only people coming to the island now were sailors and soldiers, not tourists.

David smiled his movie-star smile. "Anyway, now I can help Uncle Sam by delivering important messages!"

"That does sound like an essential job," Nanea said.

"I wish I could do more." David picked up his books. "Two more guys from my class have joined up."

Mary Lou nodded. "Every day they announce the names at school."

"You're doing plenty," Mom said to David. She kissed him good-bye. "I'll keep some supper warm for you."

Nanea could hear the engine of David's old jalopy revving up as she finished her toast. She knew Mom didn't like it when David talked about his classmates who had enlisted in the Army.

After Mary Lou cleared her dishes and left the kitchen, Nanea asked, "Do you worry that David will join up, too?"

Mom handed Nanea her lunch pail. "Let's not borrow trouble," she said. "Just do your best at school today."

As Nanea walked to Lily's house, she thought about the idea she'd come up with the night before as she was trying to fall asleep in her pitch-black room. She'd been thinking about the Minuteman flag. Her class wanted to work together to earn one and help the war effort. But buying War Stamps wasn't the only way to help. That's when Nanea came up with a doozy of an idea.

"I want to start a club: the Honolulu Helpers!" she exclaimed to Lily.

"Good name," Lily said. "What will the club do?"

"Help the war effort in Honolulu. We'll keep up with the bottle drive, of course," Nanea said. "And we can volunteer to work in Victory Gardens, and bake cookies, and serve meals, and even help in hospitals."

"Can I join?" Lily asked with a smile.

"Of course! And Patricia and Linda and Judy and Makana." Nanea began to list schoolmates' names.

"And Dixie?" Lily asked.

Nanea paused and scratched her neck. She had tried to be a buddy to Dixie. She had asked Dixie to join them for lunch every day that week, but Dixie had said no to every invitation and stayed inside instead. Sometimes Dixie's head was on her desk and her eyes were closed when the rest of the class came in. Dixie often yawned through the afternoon lessons. "Dixie doesn't seem like a joiner," Nanea finally said.

When they got to class, Lily handed Miss Smith a note.

"I have a dentist appointment today," she said.

"I'm sorry you'll miss the first chapter of our read-aloud," Miss Smith said. "But I hope you have a good checkup!"

The morning dragged for Nanea. She was so excited about the Honolulu Helpers. The moment the first recess bell rang, she bolted outside, gathering up her friends.

The girls loved the idea. "Can we have uniforms?" asked Makana.

Nanea hadn't thought of that. "I guess so," she said. The group talked, and they finally settled on white dresses with red neck scarves. Everyone had a white dress, and they decided they could make neck scarves.

"What will our first project be?" asked Linda. "I mean, after we make the scarves?"

Nanea *had* thought of that. "Valentine's Day is coming up. We could make cards for soldiers."

The girls all agreed. "This is going to be so much fun," said Makana.

Nanea smiled. Fun *and* a big help to the war effort.

After lunch, Lily left for her dentist appointment and the rest of the class settled in with paper and crayons for the read-aloud. Miss Smith always let them draw and doodle during read-alouds.

Miss Smith perched on her reading stool in the front of the room. "I brought this book from home since we are without a library for the time being." Miss Smith looked sad, but her voice was cheerful as she began to read.

Nanea rolled a crayon back and forth on the desk, listening to the lively story about a family with seven children.

"There are seven of us in my aunt's house," Dixie exclaimed. She stifled a yawn. "It's awfully noisy."

"I imagine it would be." Miss Smith smiled sympathetically at Dixie.

As Miss Smith read on, Nanea got caught up in the story. She jumped when Miss Smith closed the book.

"We'll leave it there until Monday," Miss Smith said. "But you may have five more minutes to finish your drawings before we move on to math."

Nanea added the final touches to her picture. She'd drawn three girls under the mango tree in her backyard, each reading a book. One of them was blowing a big pink bubble. Nanea decided she'd send the drawing to Donna. As she put her crayons away, she looked over at Dixie's desk. She'd drawn a picture of Mickey Mouse. It was good, even if it was kind of lopsided.

Dixie finished coloring in the ears and then wrote "Make Mickey happy. Buy War Stamps" at the bottom.

"What's that?" Nanea asked.

Dixie added a red bow tie. "A poster for the classroom. It's to get kids to buy War Stamps."

"But Lily always does the art for our classroom." Nanea snatched the drawing away. She didn't want Dixie taking Lily's job.

Dixie grabbed the drawing back, and a big corner of Mickey's ear tore off. "My poster!"

"Nanea. Dixie." Miss Smith's voice was stern. "Out in the hall."

Nanea had never been sent to the hall. She'd never been in trouble at school before—not until Dixie arrived. And now here she was in trouble the first week back at school.

Miss Smith sat Dixie on the floor on one side of the classroom door and Nanea on the other. "I certainly didn't expect this sort of trouble from either of you." Miss Smith looked at Nanea, and Nanea felt sick with shame. Miss Smith was disappointed in her. What if she sent a note home? Mom and Papa would be disappointed in her, too.

"Please tell me what happened," Miss Smith said.

"I wanted to help the class win the Minuteman flag," Dixie said. "I thought a poster would remind everyone to bring in their dimes to buy War Stamps, so I made one."

"I see." Miss Smith nodded. "That sounds like a fine goal, don't you think, Nanea?"

"But *Lily* is the class artist," Nanea said. "She should make the poster." Nanea felt another crab-pinch of jealousy. She wished she'd thought of Dixie's idea.

"It seems to me that we have room for more than one artist," said Miss Smith. She bent down toward Nanea. "Is there something you'd like to say to Dixie?" she asked kindly.

Nanea tugged at the hem of her dress. "I'm sorry about your poster," she said.

"Maybe we can tape that piece back on," Dixie said.

"All right, girls." Miss Smith stood up. "I know I can count on you to get along from here on out. Let's go back to class."

The girls stood, and then Miss Smith turned and put her arm around Dixie's shoulder.

Tears stung Nanea's eyes, and she bit her lip to keep from crying. As Miss Smith walked Dixie back to her desk, Nanea went to the supply cupboard to get the cellophane tape. She could tape Mickey's ear back together, but she didn't know how to fix the trouble she had gotten into.

Tootsie Pop Wishes

☙ CHAPTER 4 ☙

The next morning, Nanea stood outside her grandmother's *lanai*, waiting for *Tutu's* invitation to hula class. She hadn't told anyone about the poster problem, and it weighed her down like a big boulder.

"*Makaukau?*" Tutu asked the girls if they were ready to dance.

Nanea answered, *ae*, yes, along with the other dancers, but she didn't feel ready. She was still so upset about what had happened the day before that she miscounted the number of *kaholo* steps during the warm-ups. And she started with her hands down instead of at her head for "Sweet Leilani."

Tutu stopped the music. "Hula isn't just about moving one's hands and feet," she said gently. "It's about telling a story." She looked thoughtfully into Nanea's eyes. "Your mind must be on the story," she advised before starting the music again.

Nanea felt her face turn pink.

After class, as the other girls gathered their things, Nanea thought about telling Tutu about the incident at school. But before she could say anything, a car horn honked out front. It was David, there to take them to Pono's Market. Nanea worked at her grandparents' store every Saturday now, and she even helped out a few days after school, too.

As Nanea climbed in the backseat, David helped Tutu into the car. Then he got behind the wheel. "One good thing about working for Uncle Sam," David said as he drove, "is getting extra gas rations!"

People were driving less and walking more or taking the bus, because gasoline was now being rationed on the islands. It was another change because of the war.

When they arrived at the market, David helped Tutu out of the car. "Thank you," Tutu said.

"Have a good day at work, David," added Nanea.

"You, too, Monkey," David said. He hopped back in his jalopy and drove off.

"*Aloha!*" Nanea's grandfather called out the minute Nanea and Tutu stepped inside the market. "There's our famous girl!" *Tutu Kane* gestured toward the wall above the cash register where he had posted a copy of the newspaper article about Nanea and her friends.

Nanea cringed as she tied on the Pono's Market apron that her grandparents had given to her for Christmas. What would her family say if they knew she'd gotten in trouble at school? "I'll start dusting," she said, quickly moving away from the front counter.

Nanea started pulling cans and jars from a nearby shelf. She was cleaning with a feather duster when the bell over the front door jingled. Tutu and Tutu Kane were busy, so Nanea helped one customer find Saloon Pilot crackers and another find fishing line. After that, Mr. Lopez from the bakery next door came in for baking powder.

"You've got a good helper," Mr. Lopez told Tutu Kane.

"Don't I know it!" Nanea's grandfather agreed.

Between customers, Nanea put the canned goods back on the dusted shelves. She thought about Dixie and the Mickey Mouse poster on the classroom bulletin board, torn ear and all.

When Tutu Kane locked up the store at five o'clock, Tutu admired Nanea's work. "My, you'd think this was a fancy Piggly Wiggly grocery store with these sparkling shelves." Tutu gestured toward the jars of penny candy. "Such hard work deserves a reward."

Nanea chose a grape Tootsie Pop and slowly pulled off the wrapper.

"You've been awfully quiet today," Tutu Kane observed

as he flipped through receipts. "Everything okay?"

"I miss Donna." Nanea ran her tongue over the ridge in the middle of the sucker. "Sometimes I even think I smell her bubble gum."

Tutu sighed. "It is hard when someone you love is far away." She turned to tap the article on the wall behind her. "What Miss Allen said is so true. This war has been hardest on you children. You don't deserve such grown-up worries." She straightened a display of postcards on the counter. "That's why Tutu Kane and I are so impressed with all you're doing. You're managing the bottle drive, dancing at the USO shows, helping here at the market, and now you've started the Honolulu Helpers. All that and you're still such a good student. We're so proud of you."

Nanea winced. She couldn't stand it anymore. She had to tell somebody. "You wouldn't be proud of what I did yesterday," she confessed.

"Oh?" Tutu stopped straightening.

Nanea told her what happened. "I wanted Lily to do the class art like she always does." Nanea wiggled her bare toes.

"I see," Tutu said softly. "It was another unexpected change, wasn't it?"

Nanea nodded slowly. Then she lowered her voice to a whisper. "I don't think I'm Miss Smith's right-hand girl anymore." She told her grandparents about seeing her teacher put an arm around Dixie's shoulder.

Tutu's face was kind. "That's the wonderful thing about love," she said. "There's always enough to go around. When Mary Lou was born, I loved David just as much as ever. And when you arrived, that didn't change my love for your brother or your sister." Tutu patted her chest. "Hearts can grow big enough for all the people in our lives. It's the same for teachers as it is for tutus."

"That's true," Tutu Kane said. "And something else is true, too. Dixie has had a big change, moving to a new home and a new school."

Nanea dropped her head. "I suppose everything is different for Dixie."

Tutu Kane pointed at the newspaper clipping on the wall. "You have your story, *keiki*. Dixie has her own. Maybe you could discover what it is."

"Do you think she will let me?" Nanea asked.

"I think you should try," Tutu Kane answered.

Nanea waved the Tootsie Pop as if it were a magic wand. "May I take one of these for Dixie to show her I want to be her friend?"

"Good idea." Tutu opened the lid on the candy jar. "And take one for Lily. Old friendships are sweet, too."

🌺

On Monday morning, Nanea was first in line to buy a War Stamp. Dixie had been given the job of War Stamps monitor, so she collected the money. After Nanea gave Dixie the dime she'd earned from working at Pono's Market, Nanea said, "Would you like to have lunch with me and Lily today? Please?"

Dixie looked surprised, but she said yes.

When the lunch bell rang, the girls went outside and sat at a table in the shade. Instead of opening her lunch sack, Dixie sat rubbing her eyes.

"Do you feel okay?" Nanea asked.

Dixie pushed her lunch sack away and rested her head on her arms. "I'm too tired to eat," she said.

Lily nodded. "Sometimes I have a hard time sleeping because of the blackouts, too. I lay awake listening for the sounds of planes," she confessed.

Nanea agreed. "The grown-ups tell us not to worry, but how can we help it?" She thought about all the nights she tossed and turned, wondering if there would be another attack.

Dixie lifted her head. "That used to be my problem," she said. "But now I can't sleep because I have to share a room with my three little cousins. They're too young to go to school. They think we're having a pajama party every night." Dixie yawned again.

"I remember when Tommy was a baby," Lily said. "He kept us awake a lot."

"Dad says housing is hard to find and that my aunt is good to take us in, so I don't want to complain." Dixie half-heartedly opened her lunch sack, pulled out a banana, and began to peel it. "But there's something else," she sighed.

"You can tell us," Nanea said.

"It's hard being at my aunt's for another reason. She's my mom's sister." Dixie set the banana down. "Every time I look at her, I see my mom, and that makes me miss her."

Nanea and Lily exchanged glances. Neither one of them knew what to say. Finally, Nanea said softly, "Where is your mom?"

Dixie put the uneaten banana back in her lunch sack. "She won a singing contest when I was five years old. The prize was a ticket to Los Angeles to try out for a movie. She's been there ever since." Dixie looked at Nanea. "I guess she likes being in the movies better than she likes being a mom."

Nanea set down her own sandwich. "That's really sad," she said.

Lily gave Dixie a sweet rice cake from her lunch. "Have my *mochi*," she said.

"It's hard that she's so far away," Dixie admitted. "We write to each other every week, and once in a while we talk on the phone." Dixie looked at the mochi sadly. "I'm supposed to go visit her this summer, but now, because of the war, my dad says that may not happen."

The girls finished their lunches without saying much. Then they picked up their wrappers and bags and started walking to the playground. "Wait," Nanea said. She pulled a purple Tootsie Pop from the bottom of her lunch pail and handed it to Dixie. "I really am sorry about the poster."

"I know," Dixie nodded. She unwrapped the sucker. "Thanks. Grape's my favorite."

Nanea handed a red Tootsie Pop to Lily. "Would you like to join the Honolulu Helpers?" Nanea asked Dixie.

"We're going to do all kinds of things for the war effort," Lily explained. "But we're going to have a lot of fun, too."

"Count me in!" Dixie said, racing ahead to the swings. Lily was right behind her.

Nanea followed. Tutu Kane was right. Dixie did have her own story. A sad one. Nanea wondered if there was anything she could do to make it happier.

New Tricks

🐚 CHAPTER 5 🐚

Nanea was almost home when she saw Mr. Cruz, the postman, at her mailbox. "Mail for Miss Nanea Mitchell," he called.

Nanea ran as fast as she could with her gas mask and book bag. "Thank you!" It was a letter from Donna. Finally! Nanea plopped down on the porch as Mele bounded around from the back of the house to greet her. Nanea tore the letter open and began to read.

Meow, Nanea,

I'm writing this on the boat. It's our second day out, and this is nothing like the trip we took coming to Honolulu. There are no fancy dinners or movies or shuffleboard games on the deck. Last night, we had a lifeboat drill at one in the morning! I heard some sailor say it was because there were submarines in the area. Mom says not to listen to idle chatter. But wouldn't a sailor know about things like that? I can't wait to reach San Francisco.

I miss you and Miss Smith and everyone at school.

Kittens forever,

Donna

Nanea read the letter a second time and then folded it back into the envelope. Here she'd thought Donna's trip to San Francisco would be so glamorous. Nanea wrapped her arm around Mele. "Poor Donna. That sounded scary." She gave Mele a squeeze and then stood up. "Let's go answer her right now."

Nanea grabbed a couple of cookies from the kitchen and then went to her room and got out paper and a pencil. "How about some music while we write?" she asked. Mele wagged her tail.

There had been a lot of sadness that day with Dixie's story and Donna's letter. "We need something cheerful, I think." Nanea moved a bag of Mary Lou's yarn and put on the recording of "My Little Grass Shack." She sat down on the bed, humming as she picked up her pencil. *February 9, 1942. Dear Donna,* Nanea started, but Mele's scampering caught her eye. She seemed to be bouncing back and forth to the music.

Nanea put down the pencil. "Can you twirl?" she asked, standing up and moving her hand in a circle. Mele cocked her head, watching Nanea's hand. "Oh, I know!" Nanea broke off a bit of cookie and held it as she made a clockwise circle in the air. Mele lifted her nose, following the circle. "Good girl!" Nanea fed Mele the cookie. "Can you go the other way?" She broke off another chunk of cookie and moved her hand counterclockwise. Mele turned the other way and was rewarded again.

"You're getting the hang of this," Nanea said. She circled her hand clockwise and counterclockwise. Every time Mele turned in the proper direction, she got a cookie treat. "You are one smart dog," Nanea said, feeding Mele the last bite. She brushed the crumbs from her hands. "I better get to work on this letter if I want to finish it before dinner." She sat back down and began to write.

I hope you are safe and sound in San Francisco. Your trip to California sounds awful. But I have news that should help you feel better. My mom has invited your dad to dinner every Thursday. We will treat him like family—except he won't have to do the dishes.

Mele nudged at Nanea's hand, making her smudge the next word. "Mele, what are you doing?" Nanea looked at her dog. "The cookies are all gone." Mele turned in another circle. "Do you still want to dance?" Mele pawed at Nanea's leg. "Okay. Okay. Let me finish this."

You aren't going to believe this, but Mele keeps interrupting me. She wants to dance! I know it sounds crazy, but I've already taught her to twirl in both directions.

Mele pawed at Nanea again. "All right!" Nanea put her pencil down. "Let's take it from the top."

By the time Mom called Nanea to the kitchen to set the table for dinner, Mele had done so much twirling that she was ready for a nap. She curled up on Nanea's pillow and went to sleep.

At dinner, the house was as noisy as a mynah bird convention. Papa was home! He was on the graveyard shift again, which meant he would go to work after dinner, come home in time for breakfast, and then sleep during the day while Nanea, David, and Mary Lou were at school. It was the shift he used to work before the war started.

Everyone was glad that Papa was home, and everyone was talking at once. Nanea was trying to tell her family about Donna's letter when David interrupted her. "Can you pass the rice, please?" he asked.

"That's your third helping." Nanea held the rice bowl away from him.

"I'm starved, Monkey!" David pretended to grab her plate of food.

"I guess you are." Papa chuckled at David's antics. "Hard day?"

David nodded as Nanea handed him the rice. He took a heaping spoonful. "Lieutenant Gregory invited me to help the Army Corps of Engineers." Lieutenant Gregory was the Army officer David worked for, and David talked about him all the time. He said that Lieutenant Gregory was strict, but fair. "Like Pop."

David chewed and swallowed before he started talking again. "The engineers were digging trenches over by Kawaiahaʻo Church. Even though he didn't have to, Lieutenant Gregory picked up a shovel and pitched in with the rest of us." David paused. "He makes me want to do my best. To do even more."

"He sounds like quite a leader," Papa said.

David picked up his knife and cut into his chicken. "Lieutenant Gregory even let Gene come along." Gene was Lily's older brother and one of David's good friends. "He treated Gene like everyone else. He ended up hiring him," David added with admiration, "despite what happened."

"What do you mean?" Nanea asked.

"Gene went to enlist in the Army, and they turned him away," Mary Lou replied.

"They did?" Nanea asked. Gene was big and strong, like David. Why would he be turned away?

David frowned. "'No men of Japanese descent welcome,' they told him."

"I am sorry to hear that. Gene is a fine young man. He's as loyal and trustworthy as his father." Papa shook his head. "They've had it hard, what with Fudge spending so much time looking for work after his sampan was confiscated."

Fudge was Gene's and Lily's father. Nanea called him Uncle Fudge. It was hard for her to believe that anyone wouldn't trust him or the other Japanese people in Hawaii. But the Army had taken all the Japanese sampan fishing boats after the bombing of Pearl Harbor. They were worried that if enemy submarines returned to Hawaii, the Japanese fishermen on the islands would use their boats to bring spies ashore.

"I tried to get Fudge a job at the shipyard," Papa continued. "But I was also told, 'no Japanese allowed.'"

"It's a good thing Mrs. Lin gave him a job in her shop," Mom added.

"I can't wait until I'm old enough to join the Army," David said. "Then I'll enlist for Gene. That way at least someone from our 'ohana will be serving."

Nanea knew that David thought of Gene and Lily and all the Sudas as part of their family, just as she did. But she hated hearing him talk about enlisting. She pushed her green beans around on her plate.

"Anyway," David said. "Gene and I are going back tomorrow to finish digging the shelter."

"What about your schoolwork?" Mom asked.

David set down his fork. "Mom, what does math matter when there's a war on?"

"Education always matters," Mom said.

"I just want to do something," David said. "Something more than running messages."

Mom's coffee cup rattled in the saucer. "You're not eighteen."

"I will be in four months." David ran his hands through his dark hair. Beautiful hair that Uncle Sam would shave off if David went into the Army.

"I'm proud of you for being such a good friend to Gene," Papa said. "But your mother's right. We've got time before we need to talk about this."

Mom folded up her napkin. "Who's ready for dessert?" she asked.

No one said much as they ate their pineapple upside down cake. Nanea and Mary Lou washed the dishes without their usual conversation. Then it was time to get ready for the blackout.

After two months, Nanea was almost getting used to the pitch-black nights with the dark curtains drawn tight so no light escaped. Tonight Nanea sat on the sofa, thinking. She felt like a tiny pebble being tumbled in the huge waves of her brother's words. *He's going to enlist when he's old enough,* Nanea thought. *And there's no way I can stop him.*

Dogs for Defense

More than a week passed and David didn't say anything else about enlisting. Nanea went to school and did her homework and practiced for the next USO show. She worked at Pono's Market, and she and Lily and Dixie collected bottles together. The Honolulu Helpers had their first meeting, and Nanea's neighbor, Auntie Rose, helped them make red neck scarves. Then they made valentine cards for the soldiers.

Even though she tried to forget about David, Nanea's worry about him was winding itself into a bigger and bigger knot in her stomach, like one of Mary Lou's balls of yarn. Nanea hadn't been able to stop Donna from leaving. She didn't have much hope of stopping David from leaving either.

Nanea was distracted at school. During current events, Flora Bradley said something about building model planes and being an aircraft spotter, but Nanea didn't really listen.

The minute Flora finished speaking, Albert Hanson waved his hand. "My current event is about my dog, Tarzan," Albert began. "He got invited to go through some tests over the weekend. Uncle Sam is looking for dogs to help in the war. Any kind of dog." He jabbed his thumb at Teddy Fan. "Even a mutt like yours. They train them to be patrol dogs and messengers and even how to track enemy soldiers."

"Nifty!" Teddy exclaimed.

Nanea ran her finger around and around the hole in her desk where bottles of ink used to sit in the olden days. That didn't sound nifty. Dogs belonged with their families!

"And Tarzan did such a good job that the guy in charge said, 'Welcome to the Army.'"

Billy Patrick's hand shot in the air. "You enlisted?"

"Naw. Tarzan did." Albert stuck his hands in his pockets. "I'll miss him, but it's important that he's helping, right?"

"We're very proud of your contribution to the war effort, Albert." Miss Smith turned a warm smile in his direction.

"Well, the Army needs more dogs, but they won't find any as smart as Tarzan, that's for sure," Albert answered.

Albert sat down, and the class buzzed about Tarzan joining the Army. Nanea felt very hot all of a sudden. She'd been miserable the whole time Mele was missing after the Pearl Harbor attack. It was the worst two weeks of her life! If Mele joined the Army, Nanea's dog could be gone for months. Years! It was hard enough to think of David wanting to enlist! The thought of Mele leaving again was making Nanea dizzy.

"Are you okay?" Dixie asked. "Your face is all red."

"I just need some water," Nanea said. She raised her hand for permission to go out to the hall for a drink.

When Nanea returned to the classroom, she found paper and crayons on her desk. Miss Smith was starting read-aloud time. When her teacher finished reading the chapter, Nanea discovered that she'd covered her paper with doodles of dogs. Dogs with big brown eyes.

🌺

After school, Lily came to Nanea's house to plan their next Honolulu Helpers project. When they opened the front door, the girls were hit with the aroma of cinnamon and ginger.

"Hello, girls." Mom set a plate on the kitchen table. "Have a cookie." Mele hopped up on her hind legs, sniffing. "Not you, Mele," Mom scolded.

"Thanks, Aunt May," Lily answered.

"Thanks," Nanea said, taking a cookie. But she didn't eat it. She looked at Mele, and all she could think about was Albert giving up Tarzan. Nanea wrapped the cookie in a napkin and said, "Let's go to my room. I have something to show you. Come on, Mele."

Nanea closed the door to her room and went over to the phonograph player next to Mary Lou's bed. She lowered the needle and began dancing *lele* steps forward and back. Mele started moving along with Nanea.

"Look at Mele!" Lily exclaimed. "She's dancing, too."

"Good dog," Nanea said. She broke off a tiny bit of her cookie. "Forward and back," she said. Mele followed Nanea's hand and was rewarded with the sweet treat.

Lily laughed. "Is this what you wanted to show me?"

Nanea nodded, swaying her hips. Mele swayed, too.

"When did this start?" Lily asked.

"Last week." Nanea broke off another chunk of cookie for Mele. "It started with turns, and now she wants to do everything I do! So I've been teaching her."

Lily looked surprised. "Well, you're a good teacher, and Mele is a smart dog. Albert was bragging about Tarzan, but this is just as neat as helping Uncle Sam."

Nanea's light mood grew heavy at Lily's words. She took the needle off the record and hugged Mele close. "I know Mele's as smart as Tarzan," she said. "But I don't see how I could ever give her up. Not after already losing her once." She sat on the floor with Mele in her lap.

Lily sat next to them. "That would be hard," she agreed.

"And there's something else." Nanea told Lily what David had said about enlisting. "I'm worried that he will join up, like those other boys at school."

Lily sighed. "He can't enlist yet, right?"

"Right," Nanea said halfheartedly.

Lily wrapped her arm around Nanea's shoulder and gave a squeeze. "Nobody knows what will happen between now and June."

Nanea nodded. But she wished she *did* know what would happen to one dancing dog and one brave big brother.

On the last Friday of February, when she got home from school, Nanea found a second letter from Donna in the mailbox. She ran to her room, Mele right behind her, and tore it open.

Meow, Nanea,

We are finally settled in. My aunt and uncle fixed up an attic room in their house just for me. It's got blue checked curtains and a blue chenille bedspread. They remembered my favorite color, which was so very kind of them. But I'm having a hard time sleeping with city noise rather than geckos and mynah birds. Also, I keep expecting Dad to walk in the door any minute. I want us to be a family again. Mom says we have to be brave. But sometimes I can't help crying. The kids at my new school seem nice, but I miss you and Lily so much. Every night I wish on the first star I see that the war will end

soon and the Three Kittens can be back together.
   Your friend,
   Donna

Mele sniffed the letter in Nanea's hands. "Oh, she
sounds so sad," Nanea said. Donna's letter felt like another
brick on Nanea's wall of worries. Mele. David. Donna.
Nanea felt like curling up on her bed and having a good
cry. Instead, she put on "My Little Grass Shack"—Mele's
favorite—and they danced, telling the familiar story of
longing for home. Mele licked her lips when Nanea sang
the line about fish and *poi*.

When the song ended, Nanea felt lighter. Despite her
worries, dancing with Mele had brightened her spirits. *The
Army can have Dogs for Defense,* Nanea thought. *I have a dog
that can dance!*

Explosions in the Night

In the early hours of March fourth, a bad dream about David falling into a very deep hole caused Nanea to stir. Then she heard *boom-boom-boom!*

Mary Lou jumped out of bed. "What was that?" The bedroom windows rattled.

"Is it another attack?" Nanea's legs barely held her as she got up and felt her way across the room in the dark. Just three days earlier there'd been an air-raid drill. There had been many since December seventh. But Nanea knew this wasn't a drill. Not with explosions!

"To the shelter," Papa called. Nanea was so grateful he was working the day shift for a while so that he was home in the middle of the night. She couldn't imagine getting through this without him.

Nanea grabbed Mele. "Where's David?"

"Here!" In the darkness, Nanea could hear her brother hopping in the hall, trying to pull on his dungarees and run at the same time. "Did anyone hear the air-raid siren?"

"No, but let's not take any chances," Mom said.

Papa ushered them all out to the pitch-black yard.

Nanea couldn't see any stars in the cloudy sky. That made her feel even more frightened.

Once in their air-raid shelter, Papa lit a small lamp.

"I heard three booms." Nanea pulled a whimpering Mele onto her lap.

"Me, too." Mary Lou grabbed Nanea's hand.

Nanea listened hard, waiting for another explosion. Mele quivered in her arms. "You poor baby," Nanea murmured. "I know you don't like it in here. I don't, either." This dark place had to remind Mele of the hole she'd been stuck in after the Pearl Harbor bombings. "I won't let anything happen to you," she promised.

Heart pounding, Nanea leaned against her mother. She stroked Mele's head as Mom pulled her close. Nanea couldn't stop the questions from going through her mind. *What had been bombed? Was anyone hurt? When was this horrible war going to be over?*

"Does anyone hear planes?" Mary Lou asked.

"Nope," David said. "And I don't hear any fire truck or ambulance sirens, either," he added. "So it doesn't sound like anyone's been hurt."

Nanea hoped David was right.

Just then the all-clear sirens clamored through the night, signaling that it was safe to leave the shelter.

Papa picked up Nanea and Mele and carried them into

the house. "Try to get some sleep," he said as he tucked Nanea into bed. She heard the rattle of David's jalopy engine. "Where's David going?" she asked.

Papa smoothed the blanket over her. "To see if he can be of any help to Lieutenant Gregory. If there were bombs, there's bound to be cleanup."

"But won't David get arrested for being out after curfew?" Nanea asked.

"He has a pass," Papa assured Nanea. He bent to kiss her forehead. "Don't you worry. Your brother can take very good care of himself."

After Papa left, Nanea patted her pillow. Mele climbed up and slept next to her. But that didn't calm Nanea's worries. She wished David had never gone to work for Lieutenant Gregory. Then her brother would be home in his bed. Safe and sound. Nanea tossed and turned, thinking she'd never fall asleep, but she was so worn out, she finally did.

Nanea woke to the smell of Portuguese sausage. She pattered to the kitchen table with Mele at her heels.

"Good morning, Sunshine," Papa said.

Nanea yawned. "Do we know what happened last night?"

Mary Lou shook her head. "Not yet."

"There should be more news soon, on the radio," Papa added.

Nanea took a sip of juice. "Is David back yet?"

"He's still with Lieutenant Gregory," Mary Lou said, salting her eggs.

At that moment, David burst through the front door. "Well, they missed this time," he exclaimed.

"What are you talking about?" Mary Lou asked.

Mom handed David a cup of coffee and then sat down next to Nanea at the table.

"We found three craters near Roosevelt High School, on the side of Mount Tantalus," David said.

"Any damage?" Papa asked.

"At the school. Some shattered windows." David took a sip of coffee. "On the mountainside, there are a bunch of broken trees and one big bomb crater."

"Does the Army know what happened?" Mary Lou asked.

"It looks like there were two planes, with two bombs each. Remember how cloudy it was last night? Lieutenant Gregory says they had to drop their bombs blind. They missed any important targets, so there was no real harm done."

Nanea pushed the fried egg around on her plate. "Will they come back?"

"Not likely, Monkey," David said confidently. He took another sip of coffee. "Lieutenant Gregory called it a nuisance raid. He said the Japanese came back to cause trouble but that Pearl Harbor's not likely to be worth their effort anymore."

Papa's job was at Pearl Harbor. Donna's father's, too. *Are they in danger every time they go to work?* she wondered.

Mom scraped her chair back. "I'm going to listen to the radio," she said, walking into the living room.

"Why were we worth the effort the first time?" Nanea asked.

"It's complicated," said Papa.

"I'm not a baby," Nanea said crossly. She knew her father wanted to protect her, but sometimes not knowing was worse than knowing. "I can understand things, even if they're complicated."

David looked at Papa, and Papa nodded.

"You're right, Monkey," David said. "You are old enough to understand." David pulled out a chair and sat down. "Before the December attack, we had all our ships and planes in one place, Pearl Harbor, like this." David arranged the jam jar, salt and pepper shakers, and sugar bowl in the center of the table. "The Japanese attacked us there to destroy America's fleet and our ability to fight back." Then David pushed the dishes apart. "Now we've separated the ships and planes. That means Oahu's no longer such a valuable target to the Japanese. It's a whole different ball game."

Mom called from the living room. "The radio says school's on today."

"That must mean there's nothing to worry about." Papa's voice was strong and calm.

Nanea wanted to believe him, but worry still clung to her like a sticky vine.

No Laughing Matter

CHAPTER 8

I'm going to faint!" Dixie shouted.

Lily studied the book she was holding. "It says here in the Junior Red Cross Handbook that you're not supposed to let the patient look at her own injury." She held the book out to Nanea.

"I'm trying to keep her from looking," Nanea said with exasperation. The Honolulu Helpers were at the Red Cross for first-aid training, but it was not going well.

"I'm wounded, oh gadzooks, I'm wounded," Dixie declared, throwing an arm across her forehead.

Mrs. Sroat from the Red Cross frowned over at the girls. Nanea was doing her best to wrap Dixie's pretend wound the way Mrs. Sroat had instructed, but Dixie was squirming.

"Give me another bandage, please!" Nanea said to Lily. Then she turned to Dixie. "Be serious, will you?"

"Sorry." Dixie tugged at her red kerchief. "I was just trying to make it fun."

"But this is important," Nanea said sternly. "We are trying to earn our first-aid certificates."

Lily handed a length of white gauze to Nanea. Nanea looked over at Judy, who had created a complicated criss-cross wrap on Alani's hand. Nanea tried to copy what Judy had done.

"This can't be right," Nanea said. Her wrap looked like a gigantic cocoon.

Mrs. Sroat inspected Nanea's work. "There is a great deal of silliness in this corner of the room," she said. "Try again."

Nanea did try again, this time on Lily, who was a much calmer patient. It helped that she didn't wiggle and giggle as much as Dixie, but Nanea was still having a hard time getting the bandage right.

Nanea's mother appeared. She had been teaching first-aid classes at the Red Cross for months. When she saw the bandage on Lily's hand, she rolled up her sleeves. "Let's not give up yet," she said.

Half an hour later, Nanea, Dixie, and Lily had all mastered the basic bandages. "Here are your first-aid certificates," Mrs. Sroat said. She shook her head at the girls. "I wasn't sure about you three, but you managed to work together after all. Well done."

Later that afternoon, Lily and Dixie came over to Nanea's house for supper. It was Thursday, so Donna's dad would be there, and Dixie's dad was coming, too. So was Lieutenant Gregory. "The more the merrier," Mom had said.

A pan sat cooling on the counter. Dixie sniffed appreciatively. "Coconut cake!" she exclaimed. "My aunt doesn't do much baking."

"It sounds like she has quite a houseful to cook for," Mom said, trimming the ends from some green beans. "You girls can go play now. I'll call you later to set the table."

When Nanea, Lily, and Dixie stepped into Nanea's bedroom, Dixie stopped. "Wow. You only have to share a room with one other person." She sighed. "You're so lucky."

"I guess I am," Nanea admitted.

"Trust me." Dixie nodded her head. "You are."

"Does Mele have any new tricks?" Lily asked.

"Tricks?" Dixie asked.

"Wait until I show you!" Nanea put the record of "My Little Grass Shack" on the player. Then she opened a dresser drawer, pulled out a package wrapped in wax paper, and removed a cookie. "Watch!"

As the music played, Nanea performed a kaholo right, with her right thumb up as if she was hitching a ride. Then she stepped kaholo left. Mele followed her from side to side. Nanea broke off a piece of cookie, and at the sight of the treat, Mele began to turn circles.

"Oh my gosh!" Dixie cried. "Mele is dancing!"

Nanea smiled. When the music ended, Nanea rewarded Mele with another bite of cookie and lots of praise.

"You taught her all those steps in the last week?" Lily asked.

Nanea nodded. "We've been working hard."

Dixie stroked Mele's head. "That dance is so cute. Have you shown anyone else yet?"

"No," Nanea said. "I'm planning to surprise David with a performance at his birthday *luau* in June."

"I don't think you should wait that long," Dixie replied. "A hula dog is too cute to keep under wraps."

Before Nanea could answer, Mom called her to set the table and the girls rushed off, all humming "My Little Grass Shack."

"It's my favorite night of the week!" Mr. Hill announced when Nanea opened the door. Donna's dad said that every Thursday when he came for dinner.

Nanea introduced Mr. Hill to Dixie.

"My, you're a lucky girl to have friends like Nanea and Lily," Mr. Hill said. "They made my Donna feel right at home when we moved here."

Nanea blushed to remember she hadn't made Dixie feel at home right away. But Dixie just grinned.

"I sure miss her and her mom," Mr. Hill said, rubbing his chin. "The house is empty and lonely, and I can't finish any of my crossword puzzles without Donna's help." His smile was tinged with sadness.

Nanea wanted to say something to make Mr. Hill feel better, but she didn't know what words to use. She hated the war for separating families. And friends.

A few minutes later, Mr. Moreno and Lieutenant Gregory arrived at the same time. Dixie introduced her father to everyone, and then David introduced his guest, who was so tall that he looked like a coconut palm in a room full of bonsai trees. Lieutenant Gregory's close-cropped hair was strawberry blond, a shade less red than Papa's.

"I am so pleased to meet you both." Lieutenant Gregory shook hands with Mom and Papa. "And I'm grateful for this chance to tell you in person what a wonderful young man David is."

Papa smiled, and his chest puffed up like rising dough.

"We are very proud of him," Mom said. "Proud of all of our children." She wrapped an arm around each of her daughters.

"You must be Mary Lou." Lieutenant Gregory tipped his hat. Then he turned to Nanea. "And Monkey," he said. "I've heard all about you."

Nanea wanted to hide. Did the lieutenant really think

her name was Monkey? "It's nice to meet you," she replied politely.

When everyone was gathered at the table, Mele settled under Nanea's feet. She was on her best behavior and didn't beg for food. Nanea rewarded her with several green beans when Mom wasn't looking.

"Minneapolis must be so interesting," Mary Lou said to Lieutenant Gregory.

"Michigan, right?" Dixie said. They'd been learning major cities of the United States in class.

"Minnesota," whispered Nanea.

"Minnesota!" Dixie corrected her guess.

"Minnesota's home," Lieutenant Gregory admitted. "But for beauty, it's hard to beat Oahu." He nodded toward the centerpiece. "We have bluebells and asters, not lovely tropical flowers like those."

As they ate, the conversation turned to the bombings that had happened the day before.

"I'm betting that's the last time the Japanese waste their time and bombs on us," Mr. Moreno said. "They've got bigger fish to fry in the Pacific."

"It was rough to learn the Japanese just captured Singapore," Mr. Hill added.

"And those recent attacks in Australia." Papa shook his head.

"We need a break in the Pacific," David added.

Lieutenant Gregory nodded. "I know we can turn things around. Maybe at Midway."

That very morning at school, Miss Smith had pointed out the Midway Islands on the map. They were halfway between North America and Asia, which is how they got their name.

"How about some more chicken, Lieutenant Gregory?" Mom asked. "Mr. Moreno?"

The other guests all took seconds, except Dixie, who announced that she was saving room for cake.

After dinner, the men went out to the lanai while Mom made coffee and Mary Lou sliced the cake. Nanea, Dixie, and Lily washed the dishes. Nanea thought of last Thanksgiving, when she and Donna and Lily had been in this kitchen together, laughing and talking as they cleaned up. That memory felt like it belonged to a different lifetime.

"Don't you think Lieutenant Gregory is handsome?" Mary Lou asked, placing a piece of cake on a plate. "I bet he's a good dancer," she added.

Nanea made a face. "What makes you say that?" She looked over at Lily, who rolled her eyes.

Mary Lou sighed dreamily. "He's so tall."

"Tall doesn't make good dancers," Nanea pointed out.

When the coffee was ready, Mom and Mary Lou carried

the cups while Nanea, Lily, and Dixie carried the plates to the lanai. Nanea sat by David. Mele sat at Nanea's feet, staring at her cake and whimpering.

"Not now, Mele," Nanea whispered, embarrassed. Mele's manners had been so good all evening.

Nanea moved her cake out of Mele's view, but her dog knew it was still there. Mele got up and turned in a pretty circle, just like she'd done in Nanea's room when they'd been dancing. Then Mele turned in the opposite direction.

"Well done," Lieutenant Gregory said, clapping for the trick. "That is a very talented dog!"

"Nanea's been training her," Dixie announced.

All of Nanea's family members were impressed. "Wow, Monkey," David said. "When did you have time to do that?"

Nanea was a bit embarrassed by the attention. She was also disappointed. Now her surprise for David's birthday luau wouldn't be a surprise. "We've been working on it for a few weeks," she admitted.

"She just learned how to do that?" Lieutenant Gregory was clearly impressed. "What a smart dog! Have you heard about Dogs for Defense? They're borrowing family pets for Uncle Sam," he explained.

"Like Albert's dog, Tarzan," Dixie chimed in. She filled Lieutenant Gregory in on their classroom conversation.

"It's an important program," Lieutenant Gregory said.

"The Army needs smart dogs that can be trained quickly."

Nanea froze. Was Lieutenant Gregory asking her to give up Mele?

Lieutenant Gregory stood up. "This has been a lovely evening, folks." He shook Papa's hand. "Now I've got to beat that curfew."

"We all do," said Mr. Hill. "Thanks for everything, May."

"So *'ono*! Thank you for including Dixie and me," Mr. Moreno said.

Dixie looked at Nanea and Lily. "I'll see you tomorrow."

She took her father's hand, and they followed Mr. Hill out the door.

"I better scoot, too!" Lily bounded down the front steps.

Nanea watched from the front porch as everyone left. Mele was at her side, right where Nanea always wanted her to be.

Another Chance

A week later, Nanea and Mary Lou were finishing the Saturday morning breakfast dishes. They watched from the kitchen window as David weeded the Victory Garden. The whole family had helped plant the garden, and they all helped take care of it, but David enjoyed it the most. Papa said he was carrying on the Mitchell family farming tradition. Today, Gene was helping, and he and David laughed as they worked together.

Mary Lou handed Nanea the last dish to dry. "Did you hear about the Varsity Victory Volunteers group Gene started with some of the other Japanese boys?" Mary Lou asked. "The VVVs, as they're called, are building roads and warehouses and whatever else needs doing. Anything to help the war effort."

Nanea nodded. "Lily's family is still upset that the Army wouldn't allow Gene to enlist because he's Japanese," Nanea said. "None of the Sudas would ever do anything to help the enemy!"

Mary Lou let the water out of the sink. "You know that and I know that," she said, "but lots of people don't.

The VVVs will show them. Iris and I and a bunch of our classmates are meeting this afternoon to make sandwiches for them." Mary Lou looked at the kitchen clock. "Are you ready for hula class? We need to leave soon."

Nanea hurried to her room and gathered her things, her mind swirling with what Mary Lou had said about the VVVs. Nanea knew that both Gene and David wanted to enlist. Nanea didn't want either of them to leave home and get hurt. She didn't want this war to separate her 'ohana.

"Mele," Nanea called as she followed Mary Lou out the door. As Mele trotted behind them, Nanea suddenly thought about Lieutenant Gregory. Hadn't he said that Mele was smart enough to join Dogs for Defense? Was the war going to separate her and Mele *again*?

When they arrived at Tutu's lanai, Nanea's head was full of worries. But as soon as Tutu invited the dancers to class, Nanea put her troubled thoughts aside. The peaceful-ness of the movements, the joy of the music, the discipline of the steps—each element pushed her worries farther and farther away. She got swept up in the stories they were tell-ing through their dances. Stories about lovely hula hands and hospitality and love. The more she danced, the better she felt.

"You girls are ready for the next USO show," Tutu announced after class was over. "I'm very proud of you for working so hard. You will help our soldiers take their minds off their worries for a while, and that is a beautiful gift. You are an honor to the dance."

The students gathered their things and left, and Mary Lou headed to Iris's house to make sandwiches.

"Tutu, may I practice one more dance before we go to the market?" Nanea asked. For the next USO show, Nanea's group was dancing to "Lili'u E," a song written in honor of Queen Liliuokalani. Tutu had told the class that they must be very regal when they danced, and Nanea wanted to perform it perfectly.

"Of course," Tutu said. "I have a phone call to make."

Tutu went into the kitchen and Nanea put a record on the turntable. When the music started, Nanea focused on the steps and hand motions to tell the story of the queen.

As soon as Nanea began dancing, Mele jumped up from a shady spot on the lawn. She paced around Nanea, wagging her tail. The expression on her furry face was so sweet that Nanea had to laugh. She patted her thighs, and Mele raised up on her hind legs. Nanea grabbed her front paws and danced her this way and that. Then Nanea let go, and Mele trotted forward and back before doing a doggy twirl.

"What's this?" Tutu asked, coming back out to the porch. "A dancing dog?"

Nanea froze. Tutu had told her that this dance was regal. Would she think Nanea was being disrespectful? But when she saw the smile in Tutu's eyes, Nanea relaxed. "I've been teaching Mele how to hula."

"So I see," said Tutu, putting her arm around Nanea. "It looks like Mele enjoys it. Have you enjoyed teaching her?"

Nanea nodded. "At first I didn't think I'd have time, but teaching Mele helped me get my mind off other things."

"I'm glad," Tutu said, hugging Nanea close. "We all need some fun during these trying times."

🌺

Nanea slid her dime over to Dixie and took the War Stamp in return.

"That's your sixth stamp," Dixie exclaimed. "I wish everyone bought a stamp every week." She sighed. "We're never going to earn that Minuteman flag."

Nanea was concerned. She knew everyone in their class wanted to earn a Minuteman flag in honor of the men who were fighting. Why weren't more kids buying stamps?

Dixie rubbed her eyes. "One of my cousins wet the bed again last night, and her crying woke everyone up. I don't think I've had a good night's sleep since we moved here. I'm so tired." She looked at Nanea. "Could you add up this money?" She pushed a handful of coins across the desk.

Nanea sorted the pennies, dimes, and nickels. "There's

one dollar and fifty cents here," she said.

Dixie yawned. "So that means I sold twelve stamps today?"

Nanea shook her head. "No. A dollar fifty equals ten times fifteen. You sold fifteen stamps."

Dixie grinned. "I need more sleep. Thank you for your help." Dixie closed the cash box and returned the War Stamps and money to the supply closet.

Dixie and Nanea walked back to their desks. "Are you still going to come on Saturday?" Nanea asked. The Honolulu Helpers were serving refreshments at the USO show in a few days.

"I'll be there!" Dixie exclaimed. "I promise."

"And you'll bring two dozen cookies, right?" That's what all the Helpers had agreed to.

"Two dozen," Dixie said. She snapped off a salute. "Aye, aye, sir."

Nanea let out a quiet sigh. She wanted to believe Dixie, but Dixie didn't always do what she said she was going to do. She'd promised to cut out construction paper shamrocks for the Honolulu Helpers' St. Patrick's Day party, but her little cousins got hold of the scissors and ruined the paper.

"It's so hard sharing a room with them," Dixie had explained. In the end, Nanea had to quickly cut out the

four-leaf clovers, which ended up looking more like mush-
rooms than shamrocks.

🌺

That night before the blackout, Nanea and Mom sat at
the kitchen table together. Mom drank coffee and planned
her next Red Cross training meeting. Nanea made a to-do
list for Saturday's USO show. She'd be busy performing,
so it was up to the other Honolulu Helpers to set up the
refreshments. Half the girls were bringing Kool-Aid, and
half were bringing cookies. Nanea sighed, wondering
whether she should bake some cookies just in case Dixie
didn't bring any.

"That was a heavy sigh," Mom said. She looked up from
her own to-do list.

Nanea rubbed her writing hand. "It's hard being
responsible," she said.

Mom set down her pencil and reached over to pat
Nanea's hand. "We're so proud of you for starting the
Honolulu Helpers on top of everything else you're doing.
But is it too much?" Mom looked concerned.

"No. At least it wouldn't be if people did what they
said they would do." Nanea sighed again. "People who are
supposed to be my friend. Like Dixie."

"Oh." Mom raised her eyebrows. "What's up?"

Nanea picked up her pencil and twirled it in her fingers.

"She wants to help, I know she does. But every time she says she'll do something, she doesn't. I'm probably going to have to bake her cookies for the USO show." Nanea looked straight at Mom. "Now I'm sorry I asked her to join the Helpers."

"I don't know Dixie very well yet," Mom started. "But she seems to have a good heart. I'm guessing she feels bad about letting you down. Can you give her another chance?" Mom smiled.

Nanea told Mom that Dixie shared a bedroom with her three young cousins and that she wasn't getting a lot of sleep. "She had her own bedroom back on Maui, at her tutu's house."

"That explains a lot," Mom agreed. "And I would imagine she also misses her tutu."

Nanea tried to imagine having to move away from her grandparents. Without Tutu, how would she learn hula stories? Without Tutu Kane, how would she learn about the birds and flowers of the island? But Nanea knew that Dixie missed someone even more than her tutu.

"There's something else," Nanea said. Dixie had been so matter-of-fact about her mom leaving her to become an actress. But sitting here talking with her own mom made Nanea realize how hard it must be for Dixie. "Mrs. Moreno lives in California," Nanea said. She told Mom what Dixie had shared.

"Oh, I can't imagine being so far from my children." Mom shook her head sadly.

"Do you think it means she doesn't love Dixie anymore?" Nanea asked.

"Not at all." Mom leaned closer to Nanea. "Nothing ever changes a mother's love for her child." She paused to look Nanea in the eyes. "Nothing." Mom sighed. "Moving away must have been a tough decision for Dixie's mom to make."

"I wouldn't ever want you to go away," Nanea said.

Mom smiled. "That is something you *never* have to worry about." Then her smile faded. "But this part of Dixie's story tells me that you need to be even more patient with her. Show her lots of aloha."

Nanea nodded. Until that moment, she hadn't stopped to think about everything Dixie was missing.

"I'll give her another chance," Nanea promised.

Mom smiled. "That's the best we can do for a friend."

🌺

The Honolulu Helpers looked like a flock of small white and red birds as they flitted to and fro around the USO hall in their uniforms. Nanea handed Lily the task list. "You're the captain today," she said.

"Aye, aye!" Lily replied. She rounded up the Helpers and began to assign jobs.

As Nanea turned away, she noticed Dixie running into the hall, her neck kerchief askew. She was late, but she was carrying a plate of cookies. Nanea smiled and waved to her friend and then hurried to change into her costume. The first number was "My Little Grass Shack," so she put on her red hula top printed with small white flowers and the ti-leaf skirt she'd made with Tutu's instruction.

As the first notes of the song filled the USO hall, Nanea thought of Mele. Nanea always smiled when she performed, but now she beamed thinking of her little dancing dog.

The sailors and soldiers clapped after every number. Nanea could see from their faces that Tutu was right. The hula stories were taking their minds off their worries.

When the program was finished, Nanea hurried to change and help serve refreshments. She filled a cup with Kool-Aid and handed it to the next man in line.

"You're not gonna make me wear that this time, are you?" a voice asked.

Nanea glanced up. "Tennessee!" she exclaimed. Then she blushed. The last time she'd served him punch, she'd spilled it all over his uniform, with a little help from Mele! "Don't worry. You're safe."

"Does that mean Mele isn't here?" he asked. "I was hoping to pet her."

"I'm sorry," Nanea said. "That other time was a

mistake. She's not really allowed at the performances."

Tennessee looked disappointed. "It didn't seem like a mistake to me," he said. "Seeing that dog did me a world of good. But I can understand that hula and dogs don't exactly mix."

"How is your arm?" Nanea asked.

Tennessee tugged at the sling. "Another week or so and I'll be good as new," he answered. He finished the punch and handed the cup back to Nanea. "Thanks." Tennessee put his cap back on. "I best get going."

"He looked sort of sad," Dixie said as Tennessee walked away.

"It's too bad the dancing didn't cheer him up," Lily added.

"Maybe something else would," Nanea said. "Or *someone* else."

"What do you mean?" Dixie asked.

"Tennessee wanted to see Mele," Nanea explained.

"Imagine how happy he'd be if he saw her dancing!" Lily finished excitedly.

"Exactly!" Nanea said.

Dixie nodded her head. "What a great idea."

"What's a great idea?" Tutu asked. When Nanea explained, Tutu smiled. "That will really take the men's minds off their worries. In fact, I think you and Hula Dog should perform at the USO show next Saturday."

Nanea gulped. "The one at the Royal Hawaiian Hotel?" That was such a fancy place, and the show was only a week away. Nanea was nervous, but then she thought of Tennessee. No matter what, she and Mele would be ready.

Hula Dog

Nanea went through her *'eke hula* for the third time, making sure she hadn't forgotten anything. *"Pu'ili?"* she asked.

"Check," Lily replied, touching the bamboo sticks.

"Kupe'e?" asked Nanea.

Dixie picked up the ankle decoration. "Check."

"What's this?" Lily picked up a piece of fabric that was on the floor.

"Mele's skirt!" Nanea exclaimed. "I almost forgot!"

Lily smiled. "I've never seen you so nervous."

Nanea sighed. "I *am* nervous. What if Mele forgets what I've taught her? What if we mess up?"

"You won't mess up," Dixie reassured her.

"And if you do, just keep dancing," Lily said.

"The show must go on!" Dixie added, flinging out her arms dramatically.

Nanea laughed. "Okay. I'm ready. Let's go."

David drove Mele and the girls to the hotel. Nanea had gotten peeks into the Royal Hawaiian Hotel before, when she had waited outside for David to finish working, but this was her first time inside the lobby. It was no longer being used as a hotel. The military had turned it into a place for R & R—rest and relaxation—for the servicemen. Before the war, guests had paid a lot of money to stay in the luxurious rooms. Now servicemen could stay for just a few dollars each night, enjoying the beach and free local entertainment.

"Look up there," Lily whispered as they crossed the large room.

The three girls tilted their heads back, admiring the enormous crystal chandeliers glittering overhead. Thick rugs covered the polished floors, and the elegant rattan chairs and sofas were dotted with plump, colorful pillows.

"This looks like a scene out of a movie," said Dixie.

David escorted them to the ballroom. A double row of columns carried Nanea's eye to a long bank of windows that framed blue sky and sunshine. There were rows and rows of chairs lined up like silent soldiers. Lots of people would be watching the debut of Hula Dog!

Tutu stood on the stage holding open the curtain. Nanea could see the other dancers behind the thick red drapes. "Nanea!" Tutu called out. "We're just getting ready to warm up."

"Wish us luck," Nanea said.

"Luck!" said Dixie. "But you won't need it."

"We'll be right up front," Lily added.

"Break a leg, Monkey," David said. "And I guess you should break a paw, Mele."

Tutu let the curtain fall closed behind Nanea. Mele sat in the wings, watching, while the dancers warmed up. Nanea could hear the chairs on the other side of the curtain squeak and scrape the floor as the arriving soldiers took their seats.

The lights dimmed to signal the start of the show. Nanea took several deep breaths to calm herself. But she was so preoccupied with the Hula Dog act that she got out of rhythm with her pu'ili as she danced to "Green Rose Hula." A stern look from Makana got her back on track. The song finished, and the girls bowed their heads. "You weren't paying attention," Makana whispered as they exited the stage.

"Sorry." Nanea shook her head to clear it of anything but dance steps. She ducked behind a curtain and changed her costume as quickly as she could.

"Ready?" Mary Lou asked.

"I hope so." Nanea stroked Mele's head to calm herself.

Mary Lou signaled to Tutu to introduce the act. "This is my grandson, David Mitchell," Tutu announced. "He'll be playing ukulele for his sister, Nanea Mitchell."

Nanea walked to the center of the stage. She posed, waiting.

"And this afternoon Nanea is dancing with a new partner—Mele, the Hula Dog!"

David started "My Little Grass Shack," and Mele pranced out on the stage. There were lots of chuckles and some "awws" and "good dogs."

Nanea moved her feet and hands to David's music. Mele watched, wagging her tail.

The men in the audience chuckled a little louder. That made Nanea even more nervous. David played the first few measures again.

"Mele," she said. "Dance!"

Mele shook herself from head to toe. Then she cocked her head. Nanea did a kaholo right and made the hitchhiking motion with one thumb while her other hand rested on her hip. Nanea folded her arms across her chest, and then drew an hourglass in the air with her hands.

As if that had been the cue she'd been waiting for, Mele stood on her hind legs. She pranced forward and back, side to side, turning in circles each time Nanea made a swaying motion. When David sang the last words of the song, Nanea brought her hands together, reaching them out over her pointed foot.

As if that had been the cue she'd been waiting for,
Mele stood on her hind legs.

Soldiers and sailors jumped to their feet, cheering and stamping.

After the performance, the dancers served refreshments to the soldiers on a patio overlooking the ocean. Dixie and Lily rushed up to Nanea, who was pouring punch. "You stole the show!" Dixie gushed.

Lily nodded. "Everyone is talking about Hula Dog!"

"And her talented teacher," David added, giving Nanea a thumbs-up.

"Your first solo. Almost," added Mary Lou, with a sisterly wink. "Good job."

"That was some number." Tennessee stood in front of Nanea, grinning.

"You gave me the idea," Nanea told him. "I hope seeing Mele did you a world of good," she added, echoing Tennessee's words from the week before.

"Would the star mind if I said hello?" he asked. "As soon as I saw her onstage, I was hoping I could pet her."

Nanea was surprised at how eager Tennessee sounded. "Sure. Come on."

Mele was lapping at a bowl of water, and Tennessee fussed over her like she was Rin Tin Tin.

"Almost makes me feel like I'm back home with my Blue," Tennessee said. "Whoever said dogs are man's best friend said a mouthful. Gosh, I miss that mutt."

Soon a crowd had gathered. Tennessee reluctantly stepped away from Mele, giving some of the other men the chance to get close to her.

Nanea was surprised that some of those big strong men wiped tears from their eyes after petting Mele. Almost every one of them commented about a dog they'd left behind. It made Nanea happy and sad at the same time.

Tennessee hung around until the last soldier had left. "Thanks for letting me see her," he told Nanea. He gave Mele one last scratch behind the ears. "I best be pushing off, too," he finally said.

"Aloha," Nanea called after him. Then she knelt down and wrapped her arms around Mele's neck.

"Good dog," she said. "Good, good dog."

All Fired Up

On the first day of April, Nanea pored over the newspaper as the family ate breakfast. She needed an article to take to school for current events.

"Did you see this?" Nanea pointed to a photograph of the Aloha Tower. The tower had already been painted in camouflage colors to hide it from enemy planes. But now the clock face had been painted black.

"I have seen it," David said. "It looks ugly."

"The military is doing its job," Papa said.

"I know," Mary Lou said. "But it makes me sad."

"It makes me sad, too," Mom said. "But we don't want anything to happen to the tower."

Nanea looked at the newspaper photo again. The word "aloha" was written on all four sides of the tower in big letters. "Tutu says the tower is a symbol of the aloha spirit. It's like a friendly smile welcoming everyone to Honolulu."

Mom handed Nanea a plate of scrambled eggs and rice. "They can paint the clock black," she said, "but there's not enough paint in the world to cover up the aloha spirit. We will still treat everyone with care and kindness."

"That's what Iris's family did," Mary Lou said. "Right after the bombing, they took in that lady—Trina—and her baby when her house and everything they owned was destroyed the day of the bombing." Mary Lou paused. "And her husband was on the USS *Arizona*," she added softly.

Nanea set the newspaper aside. When Pearl Harbor was attacked, so many men—thousands—had lost their lives on ships like the *Arizona*. Their families now had to go on without their loved ones.

"The aloha spirit means we share each other's joys and sorrows," Mom said softly. "No matter what."

Nanea nodded. She had given up her favorite teddy bear when Iris was collecting toys and clothes for Trina's son. That little boy would never know his father. Nanea couldn't imagine growing up without Papa. She blinked back tears.

"Look at the time," David said suddenly. Both he and Mary Lou got up from the table and cleared their dishes. "I'll be home late tonight. Work!"

"I'll be late, too," Mary Lou said, following David out the door. "I'm cooking for aid workers over at the church."

After David and Mary Lou left, Mom jumped up from the table. "They forgot their lunches!" She grabbed the paper sacks from the counter and hurried outside.

"You haven't eaten much, Sunshine," Papa said.

Nanea pushed the eggs around on her plate. "I got a letter from Donna yesterday."

"Oh?" Papa said.

Nanea put her fork down and pulled a letter from her pocket. She read it aloud.

Meow, Nanea,

Yesterday I went to school, and two of my new friends were gone. Their families have been sent away to a war relocation camp called Manzanar. It's happening to all the Japanese living on the West Coast, not just here. Susie and Emi were the first people to invite me to sit with them at lunch. At first I wanted this war over so the Three Kittens could be back together. Now I also want it over so Susie and Emi can come home.

Your friend,

Donna

Nanea looked at Papa. "It was bad enough when Uncle Fudge got sent away. He was a grown-up. Why are they sending kids away? Will they get to stay with their families?"

Papa scooted his chair away from the table and patted his knee. Nanea went to sit on it, leaning her head against Papa's chest.

"I don't agree with it, but the Army has decided that for the safety of the country and the safety of Japanese Americans, it's best that they be moved," he said.

"But why?" Nanea asked.

"Well, Japan is directly across the Pacific Ocean from the West Coast of the United States," Papa explained. "I guess the people in charge think if the Japanese military attacked that area, the people of Japanese descent living there might help them and fight against Uncle Sam."

"So it's like what the FBI thought about Uncle Fudge? That he wouldn't be loyal?" she asked.

"That's a big part of it," Papa said.

"No Japanese American I know would fight for the enemy," Nanea said.

"I agree," said Papa, "but I'm not in charge."

"Well, if I was in charge, I wouldn't make people leave their homes and schools," Nanea said. "I would believe in them."

Papa hugged her close. "I'm so proud of you. You are a fine example of the aloha spirit." Papa held her out at arm's length. "You are really growing up, Nanea. And I guess that makes sense, with a special birthday just around the corner.

Now when is it again?" he teased.

"Papa! You know. It's next Saturday," Nanea said.

"That's right. My Sunshine will be ten on April eleventh." He kissed the top of her head. "I would never forget that."

"I wonder where David is," Nanea said as she finished setting the dinner table.

"We may have to start without him." Mom took a steaming dish out of the oven.

Just then, the front door burst open and David hurried in with Lieutenant Gregory.

"Sorry we're late," David said. "Lieutenant Gregory was speaking to the Hawaii Defense Volunteers, and he invited me along." David nodded toward Lieutenant Gregory. "So I invited him to dinner."

Papa shook Lieutenant Gregory's hand. "We're glad you're here."

Mary Lou quickly set another place at the table as Mele trotted over to say hello.

"There's that smart dog," Lieutenant Gregory said, giving Mele a pat.

Nanea tugged Mele away. "Leave the company alone," she told her dog.

"Please, sit down," Mom said. "Dinner's ready."

As Papa passed the platter of fish to Lieutenant Gregory, he asked, "What did you talk to the volunteers about?"

"Their efforts, mostly," Lieutenant Gregory answered, serving himself. "I try to encourage people by letting them know that even small contributions help the war effort."

"He's a good speaker," David said. "He got people all fired up and eager to do more."

Lieutenant Gregory ducked his head modestly. "I just say what I believe."

"And you make others believe, too," David added with admiration.

Lieutenant Gregory smiled at Nanea when she passed him the bowl of rice. "How is school, Nanea? David tells me you like third grade."

"I do," Nanea said quietly. "Our class is trying to earn a Minuteman flag." She paused. "But we're not doing very well."

"You need a pep talk from Lieutenant Gregory," David said with a laugh. "That would change things."

"Nanea's certainly been doing her part," Papa said. "She's bought a stamp every single week."

Lieutenant Gregory looked impressed. "Every dime adds up," he said.

After dinner, Lieutenant Gregory excused himself before dessert. "I have to leave now if I'm going to make it back before curfew," he said. "It was a pleasure seeing all of you again. And you, too, Mele."

Mele left her place next to Nanea's chair to lean against Lieutenant Gregory's leg. Lieutenant Gregory reached down and scratched Mele's ear. "Next time I hope I'm here long enough to see your latest tricks," Lieutenant Gregory said. "You're one smart dog."

Nanea patted her leg, motioning Mele to come back to her. *She's my smart dog,* thought Nanea. *Not Uncle Sam's.*

At school the next day, Miss Smith had just finished taking attendance when there was a knock at the classroom door. "This must be our special guest," she said mysteriously.

When Miss Smith opened the door, Nanea nearly fell off her chair. It was Lieutenant Gregory!

Nanea's classmates were abuzz to have a real live officer in their very own classroom. Nanea was nervous. Was he here to talk about Dogs for Defense?

"First, I want to thank your teacher for allowing me to spend a few moments with you today." He nodded toward Miss Smith. "Now, people think that I have an important job because I'm in the Army. But do you know who has an even more important job?"

Thirty-two heads shook no.

Lieutenant Gregory drew a big circle with his hand, encompassing every student in the class. "You. And your parents. You see, Uncle Sam can't win the war without you. And it's the little things that matter most. Like your mothers saving their cooking grease to help make ammunition. Or writing a letter to a wounded serviceman." Lieutenant Gregory reached into his pocket and pulled out a dime. He held it up to the class. "Or bringing in one thin dime to buy a War Stamp." He put the coin back in his pocket. "Now, can Uncle Sam count on your help?" he asked.

"Yes, sir!" Billy shouted.

"I think Billy speaks for the class, Lieutenant Gregory," Miss Smith said.

"That's the spirit." He saluted. "I know we'll win with students like you in the fight." He smiled at Nanea and left the room.

"Wow! A real soldier!" Albert exclaimed.

"And he came here just to talk to us," said Flora.

"I'm going to bring in *two* dimes next week," Billy announced.

David was right, Nanea thought. *Lieutenant Gregory's words do get people fired up. And it must have been David who asked Lieutenant Gregory to talk to our class.*

Nanea had a feeling that on the next War Stamps day, everyone would be in line with a dime.

A Birthday Mystery

Nanea rolled over. Something was different—and it wasn't just that she was a year older. Mary Lou was already up and her bed was made. Odder still, there was a note safety-pinned to her sister's pillowcase. Nanea blinked. Her name was on it.

Nanea jumped out of bed and opened the note. *Go see Auntie Rose for your first birthday treat and your first clue.*

Nanea shook her head. What was going on? She threw on her clothes. "Come on, Mele. Let's solve this birthday mystery."

Auntie Rose's front door opened before Nanea could knock. "Happy birthday!" Auntie Rose handed over a fragrant sack, along with another note. This one said: *Get cracking to your favorite seed shop.*

That was an easy clue. Nanea pulled a sugar-coated malasada out of the sack. "Thank you, Auntie!"

"Have fun!" Auntie Rose called as Nanea bit into the warm doughnut. She and Mele raced to Mrs. Lin's. Nanea wiped her sticky fingers on her shorts before going into the store. "Wait here," she told Mele.

"Is that Sherlock Holmes I see?" Mrs. Lin pretended to look at Nanea through a magnifying glass.

Nanea giggled. "It's me! Nanea, the detective."

"Ah, then." Mrs. Lin nodded. "I have a secret message for you, Nanea the detective." She handed over a packet of *li hing mui* cherry crack seed with a note taped to the back.

Nanea read the note aloud. *"Go to the place where chocolate candy and a fragrant flower live together.* This is a tricky one."

"Think about different kinds of candy and flowers," suggested Mrs. Lin.

"Well, there are candy bars, like Baby Ruths," Nanea said. "And *pikake* and ginger flowers are fragrant."

Mrs. Lin smiled. "Keep going."

"Okay," Nanea said. "Chocolate-covered cherries, Tootsie Rolls, chocolate kisses, and—fudge!" she cried. "Fudge is a chocolate candy. And *lily* is a fragrant flower. The Sudas!"

Mrs. Lin chuckled. "You are one sharp detective."

Nanea and Mele ran pell-mell to Lily's house. Lily opened the front door to Nanea's knock.

"You'll never guess," Nanea exclaimed. "Mary Lou made a treasure hunt, and it led me here!"

Lily wiggled her eyebrows. "Oh, I might be able to guess." She opened the door wider. In the living room, Nanea could see her entire 'ohana, including Uncle Fudge

and Aunt Betty and their boys, Auntie Rose, and even
Dixie. "Surprise!" Lily cried. "Happy birthday."

Everyone crowded onto the front porch, kissing and
hugging Nanea.

Mary Lou slipped a *lei* over Nanea's head. "Happy
birthday, baby sis."

"We wanted to surprise you, Monkey," David said. "Did
it work?"

Nanea sniffed the lei. "And how!"

"Now for the best part," Tutu said. "A picnic!"

"We've saved up our gas coupons so we get to drive!"
Lily said.

Nanea, Lily, and Dixie grabbed hands and ran to
squeeze into the backseat of Uncle Fudge's car with Mele,
Tutu, and Aunt Betty. By the time the caravan pulled
away from the curb, three vehicles were filled to the brim
with people and picnic goodies. They drove to a stretch of
Waikiki Beach by the aquarium. Even with the barbed wire,
Nanea thought the beach was beautiful. After the cars were
parked, everyone got out and grabbed something to carry.

"Look!" Nanea shifted the blankets in her arms to point
toward Kapiolani Park. It was filled with junker cars spaced
out evenly like pieces on a game board. "Why did they do
that?" she asked.

"It looks terrible," added Dixie.

David explained. "It's part of the Army's plan to keep enemy airplanes from landing."

Nanea felt like she'd swallowed sand. Even on birthdays, there was some reminder of war.

"Don't worry, Monkey. It's only a precaution. No worries on this special day. I'll race you to the water!"

Mele barked and ran on the beach as all the kids splashed in the water. "Who's going to help fish for lunch?" Papa called to them, pulling out the poles.

"Me!" Nanea shouted happily. She hadn't thought of her favorite pastime in ages.

"I bet I catch the biggest one," David bragged.

"Nothing doing," said Gene. "That will be me."

They laughed good-naturedly when Lily reeled in the catch of the day.

While the fish cooked over a small fire that Papa and Tutu Kane had built, Mom produced a small stack of gifts for Nanea. Lily had made her a picture frame out of Popsicle sticks, like the one she'd made for Donna. Dixie presented her with a pair of red barrettes.

"I thought those would look pretty in your hair," Dixie said as Nanea unwrapped them.

"They will!" Mary Lou agreed.

David gave Nanea a new Nancy Drew mystery, and Mary Lou's gift was a coin purse with three kittens stitched on the front. Tutu had sewn matching pineapple-print skirts for Nanea and Mele. "A perfect fit!" Mom pronounced when Nanea tried hers on. Mele couldn't be caught to model hers. She was too busy chasing beach birds.

"This one is from your Mitchell grandparents," Papa said, handing Nanea a box. "Luckily they mailed it before Christmas to make sure it would get here in time."

"That's a good thing," Tutu said as Nanea unwrapped the package. "With the war, who knows when it would have arrived."

"A camera!" Nanea exclaimed. "And film!"

"It's just like Donna's," Lily noted.

Nanea nodded. "I can't wait to try it out!"

The last gift was from Tutu Kane. Nanea gasped when she saw the shell lei. "Oh, thank you! *Mahalo ia 'oe.*" She fastened the string of tiny shells around her neck.

"I gathered those shells from the island of Ni'ihau years ago," Tutu Kane said.

Nanea knew the story, and she knew he'd kept them until the right moment to make special leis for each of his grandchildren.

"It is time for you to wear this," Tutu Kane said. "May it grant you a safe and peaceful journey through the rest of your life."

"It's beautiful." Nanea touched her neck gently, knowing that it had taken her grandfather a long time to make such a lei. It was a treasure greater than diamonds. With it around her neck, she felt like Hawaiian royalty. Like Queen Liliuokalani.

"You are growing up full of aloha," Tutu Kane said. "And you are growing up so fast. Faster than David and Mary Lou, because of the war." Tutu Kane put his hands on Nanea's shoulders. "I gave them their leis when they each turned thirteen, not ten. But it is time for you to wear this." He hugged Nanea. "May it grant you a safe and peaceful journey through the rest of your life."

"Thank you," Nanea said. "Thank you everyone. For the gifts and for the birthday surprise."

David started strumming his ukulele, and Tutu Kane joined in. Everyone danced. Mary Lou and Dixie taught a new jitterbug step. Nanea giggled when Tutu tried it out.

"I think I should stick with hula," Tutu said, fanning her face.

"Hey!" Nanea exclaimed. "Everybody huddle up. I want to take a picture." Papa helped Nanea load the film into the camera as everyone gathered together. Then she snapped a photo of the whole group. After that, Gene and Nanea switched places so that Nanea could be in a picture.

As the grown-ups began unpacking the picnic baskets,

Nanea saw that every single one of her favorite foods was on the menu.

"I made two-finger poi." Tutu winked at Nanea. "Just the way you like it."

Nanea scooped up a taste of the thick mashed *taro* with her index and middle fingers. "So 'ono."

Papa and Tutu Kane roasted frankfurters with the fish, and there was watermelon and potato salad and birthday cake. As Nanea put her new camera carefully back into the box, she couldn't decide what made her happier—the feast her family had prepared or the fact that everyone was there to enjoy it with her.

"What are you thinking?" David asked Nanea quietly.

"I'm thinking that we are pretty lucky to be part of this 'ohana," Nanea answered.

David reached over and tugged a strand of Nanea's long dark hair. "Yes, we are. I never want to leave this place."

Nanea held those words in her heart. They were more wonderful than her birthday surprises. *David didn't want to leave! Never! So there, Uncle Sam!*

Nanea couldn't have asked for a better present.

Big Problems
CHAPTER 13

At the end of May, Nanea sat cross-legged on the living room floor with a sturdy canvas backpack in her lap. She was filling it with supplies. "I don't know why we need evacuation kits when everyone says the Japanese won't come back to attack us," she grumbled.

"The Army wants us all to have a bag packed," Mom said lightly. "In case of an emergency."

"But what kind of emergency?" Nanea asked.

"Oh, it's just part of being prepared," Mom said.

"Why isn't Mary Lou making a kit?" Nanea asked.

"I already made mine," Mary Lou said, barely looking up from her knitting. "Four days' worth of supplies."

Mom was working on her own kit.

"Where's David's?" Nanea asked. "And Papa's?"

"The Army only evacuates women and children," Mom said. "The men stay behind and help."

Nanea didn't like the sound of that. She thought of Donna's friends Emi and Susie going to the camps with their families. If Nanea had to leave her home for any reason, she wanted to go with everyone in her 'ohana.

"Let's not borrow trouble," Mom added. "We're doing this to be on the safe side."

"Don't you remember what Lieutenant Gregory told David?" Mary Lou added. "We're too far away for the Japanese to bother with anymore."

Nanea added some canned goods to her kit, which included a blanket, long pants, a sweater, a toothbrush and toothpaste, a hairbrush, soap, a towel, and a flashlight. She closed up the backpack and tried to hoist it onto her back.

"Oof!" Nanea nearly tumbled backward. "How am I going to be able to carry all this *and* a gas mask?"

"And don't forget Mele's evacuation kit." Mary Lou pointed to the small bag Nanea had made for her dog.

"Do your best," Mom rolled up some socks and slid them into her own evacuation kit.

Nanea reached into hers and pulled out two cans of peaches. She tried the backpack on again. "Much better," she said sadly. She really did love peaches.

There was a knock at the door. When Nanea opened it, Lily and Dixie were standing on the porch, and Lily was holding her bag of jacks.

"Want to play?" Lily asked.

Nanea was happy to leave thoughts of evacuation kits behind. Mom gave the girls some mountain apples. "Why don't you take them outside," she suggested.

On the front porch, Mele wandered from girl to girl, hoping for a handout.

"I've never seen a dog eat apple before," Dixie said.

"Mele likes anything her people are eating," Nanea said. "Even green beans."

David's car rattled to a stop in front of the house. He waved to the girls as he hurried up the porch with an envelope in his hand. "Mail for you," he said to Nanea.

"A letter? From Donna?" she asked.

"You're fifty percent right," he said. "It's a letter, but from Private First Class Ronald Paul. He asked me to deliver it in person." David made a silly bow and then handed her the letter.

Nanea was confused. "Who?"

David winked. "Read it and see."

Nanea tore the letter open and read it aloud.

Dear Nanea,

I'm healed up real well now, so Uncle Sam's putting me back to work. I ship out soon. But I couldn't leave without thanking you for letting me spend time with Mele. She was better than any medicine they gave me in the hospital, I can tell you that for sure.

Well, as you say in Hawaii, aloha.
PFC Ronald Paul

Below that, he'd signed, "*Tennessee.*"

"Neat," Lily said.

"Good job, Monkey." David ruffled Nanea's hair. "You, too, pup," he called to Mele as he headed into the house.

Nanea sat down on the front step and read the letter again. "This gives me an idea," she said to Lily and Dixie. "Something different for the Hula Dog act."

"It's pretty popular," Lily said, sitting down on one side of Nanea.

"Mele really cheers people up," Dixie said, sitting down on the other side of Nanea.

"Right. So what if I took Mele to visit sick and injured servicemen?" Nanea asked. "We could dance, sure, but they could also pet her and stuff like that." Nanea tapped the letter against her leg. "Tennessee said spending time with Mele was better than any medicine the hospital gave him. This could be Operation Mele Medicine!"

Dixie tugged on her ear. "That sounds good for the soldiers," she began. "But I remember when I got my tonsils out. My friends couldn't visit me in the hospital because they weren't fourteen yet. Hospitals are very strict about rules."

"We're not fourteen," Lily said.

"And she's a dog," Dixie said, pointing at Mele.

"Those are two big problems," Nanea agreed. "There has to be some way to solve them. I wonder—"

Nanea stopped talking. She heard David and Papa in the living room, and there was an urgency to David's voice that made her listen.

"Something is up," David was saying. "I've never seen so many sailors walking around downtown. There are ships as far as the eye can see off Waikiki. And I heard there's lots of activity at Hickam Field, too."

Nanea hugged her knees close. Little prickles of worry raced up and down her body.

"The scuttlebutt I hear is that it's for something in the Pacific," Papa said. "Not here. Maybe Midway."

"Daddy and Gene were talking about Midway last night," Lily whispered. "The United States has a base there, but the Japanese want to control it, they said."

"I wish I was out there," David said. "I feel so useless delivering messages."

"Delivering messages is important," Papa assured him.

"When I join up, I'll be able to do something that matters," David replied.

"What you're doing right now matters," Papa insisted. "We don't know what's happening in Midway yet."

Nanea couldn't breathe. It had been a while since David mentioned joining the Army. Nanea had hoped he'd forgotten about it. Now she knew there was no chance he would forget. This was an even bigger big problem.

There was an assembly at school the next day. In the auditorium, a row of chairs marched across one side of the stage, with a tall wooden podium in the middle. Principal Baxter and several special guests, including Lieutenant Gregory, sat facing the students.

"This is boring." Billy Cruz wiggled around in the seat next to Nanea. "With a capital B."

"Remember your manners, please, Billy," Miss Smith said.

Billy let out a big sigh when another adult got up to speak. Miss Smith gave him a stern look.

Nanea had to admit, there was a lot of talking.

Finally, Mrs. Baxter returned to the podium. "Thank you so much for those words, Mr. Ross," the principal said. "And now, for our final speaker of the assembly—"

Nanea's class applauded loudly as Lieutenant Gregory walked to the podium. He thanked Mrs. Baxter. "I am honored to be here today and proud of your patriotic support of your country. You have truly shown the aloha spirit through your participation in the War Stamps drive.

This school alone has collected enough money to buy one tank! Think of that." Lieutenant Gregory looked out over the auditorium, smiling.

"From this young first-grader here in the front row," he pointed at a girl with a bow in her hair, "to the President of the United States, every person's contribution matters. Whether you buy a stamp, invite a soldier to dinner, or loan your dog to Uncle Sam"—Lieutenant Gregory seemed to look right at Nanea—"what you do counts."

Nanea slunk down in her seat. Why did he have to bring up the part about dogs?

"Keep it up!" Lieutenant Gregory finished. He snapped off a salute to the students. "Now, one class has earned a Minuteman flag with their dedicated support of the War Stamps drive." He stepped away from the podium, picked up a folded flag, and paused. "Miss Smith, please come forward and accept this flag for your third-grade class!"

As Miss Smith stood up, Nanea saw tears glistening in her eyes. Nanea's classmates whistled and cheered, and the principal didn't even shush them.

Nanea cheered, too, because she was happy for Miss Smith and their class. But inside, she was unhappy for herself. Lieutenant Gregory's words reminded her that she stood a good chance of losing both her brother and her dog to the war.

David's Birthday

ow does this look?" Dixie held out a flower arrangement she'd made.

"Beautiful," Nanea said without looking.

Dixie's smile faded. "You don't like it," she muttered.

"Yes, I *do* like it," Nanea insisted. "I'm sorry, Dixie. I'm just distracted."

That morning, Nanea had overheard her parents talking. Mom had sounded so upset. "I'm worried that he'll go right out and enlist," Mom had said. "He's eighteen today. We can't stop him." Then Mom had started to cry.

Papa's calm voice had said, "Let's not borrow trouble, May. Besides, today is for celebrating David." Then their voices had faded, and Nanea couldn't hear anything more.

Nanea told her friends what her parents had said.

Lily sighed. "The war sure has put a dark cloud over a lot of birthday luaus."

"Remember what your dad said," Dixie encouraged. "Today is a day to celebrate David."

"I'll try." Nanea looked around the lanai and the backyard. "There's still a lot to do to get ready. Let's hang the streamers."

Dixie took one end of a streamer and sniffed the air. "That *kalua* pig smells so good. I haven't had it in so long."

Food was an important part of any luau. Nanea loved the festive dishes, especially Tutu's poi. There would be *lomi* salmon with tomatoes and onions, *laulau*—pork and butterfish wrapped in ti leaves—and of course the special recipe that the luau was named after: chicken and taro leaves baked with coconut milk. But more than the food, Nanea especially loved knowing that people in her 'ohana had been celebrating like this since she didn't even know when. In ancient times, men and women couldn't eat together. She was glad that had changed. Otherwise, she wouldn't be able to attend her own big brother's birthday party!

When the streamers were hung, Nanea sat down in the grass next to Mele. "What are we going to do about Operation Mele Medicine?" she asked, stroking her dog's ear. "How can we get you into the hospitals to cheer up wounded soldiers?"

Mele only thumped her tail.

"Maybe you need a new approach," Dixie said, sitting down on the other side of Mele. "Don't you remember

Lieutenant Gregory saying there are lots of ways to help Uncle Sam?"

"Wait a minute," Lily said. "Nanea, why don't you tell *Lieutenant Gregory* about your idea for Operation Mele Medicine? Maybe he could help."

Nanea felt a twist in her stomach. "I can't," she said. "Lieutenant Gregory wants me to give Mele up for Dogs for Defense," she blurted out.

Lily and Dixie were shocked. "When did he say that?" Lily asked.

"He's *always* asking about Mele and telling me what a smart dog she is. Remember that night at dinner?" Nanea asked. She listed all the other times Lieutenant Gregory had told her the Army needed smart dogs. "And last week at the assembly, when he brought up Dogs for Defense, he looked right at me." Nanea bit her lip to keep from crying. "I am not going to give up David *and* Mele."

Nanea's friends were quiet. Then Dixie sat up straight. "Maybe if you tell Lieutenant Gregory about Operation Mele Medicine, he would see that's a better way for Mele to help the war effort. Maybe he would even talk to someone at the hospitals and convince them to let Mele in."

"He is good at convincing people to do things," Lily agreed. "Remember the War Stamps talk?"

Nanea nodded. But she just didn't know if she could

trust Lieutenant Gregory to help her. "I have to think about it," she said.

"Sit down, please, everyone," Tutu called out later that afternoon. "We'll have some hula in honor of David's special day."

Tutu Kane played his ukulele while Mary Lou and Nanea danced the hula they'd created to celebrate David. Nanea felt proud of the way it turned out. The dance told the story of her wonderful big brother. Nanea's hands and feet talked about all David had done and all he would do. She and Mary Lou chose movements to compare him to the tallest of palm trees: strong, but able to bend in a hard wind. Each step put more distance between Nanea and her worries. After they finished, Tutu and Mom danced, too. Nanea hoped someday she would be as graceful as her mother and grandmother.

"Wonderful!" Lieutenant Gregory exclaimed when they finished. He turned to Papa. "It's an honor to be part of this special day." As Mom joined their conversation, Lieutenant Gregory said, "Everything was delicious, Mrs. Mitchell."

Mom smiled. "Can I get you another slice of pie?"

Lieutenant Gregory groaned. "Maybe just a sliver."

Dixie ran over to Nanea and Lily. "You'll never guess!" She jumped up and down. "My dad was just talking to

Donna's dad. Mr. Hill has invited us to live at his house until Donna and Mrs. Hill come home. I'll have my own room!" She clasped her hands together. "I can sleep again!"

"That's great news," Lily said.

"I'm so happy for you," added Nanea.

Mom handed a plate to Nanea. "Could you please take this to Lieutenant Gregory?" she asked.

"Now's the time to talk to him," Lily urged.

"You can do it," Dixie added.

Nanea stood tall as she and Lily and Dixie approached the lieutenant.

He took the plate. "You three look serious. What's up?"

Nanea grabbed hands with Lily and Dixie and took a deep breath. "I want Mele to help Uncle Sam."

"Dogs for Defense?" Lieutenant Gregory paused with a bite of pie halfway to his mouth. He sounded surprised. "I know how much Mele means to you—and how you've already lost her once."

Nanea was surprised. "You do?"

Lieutenant Gregory put his fork down. "The first thing David told me about his baby sister was how determined she was to find her dog." He smiled warmly at Nanea. "You didn't give up on Mele. We both admire you for that."

"But we thought you wanted Mele for Dogs for Defense!" Lily said.

"What gave you that idea?" Lieutenant Gregory asked.

"You were so interested in her that night at dinner," Dixie explained.

Lieutenant Gregory laughed. "Who wouldn't be interested in a hula-dancing dog?"

"So you don't want Mele to join the Army?" Nanea asked, squeezing her friends' hands.

"Not if you don't want her to. Dogs for Defense is an important program, but it's your decision to make. Not mine." He smiled again. "Besides, it seems she already has a big job. I hear that the soldiers love Hula Dog."

Relief washed over Nanea like a wave. "I have an idea about that," she said. "It's called Operation Mele Medicine." She told him about the letter from Tennessee. "I could take Mele to the hospitals once a week so the men could pet her and play with her."

Lieutenant Gregory frowned. "Dogs and hospitals don't exactly mix."

"Well, she doesn't have to be *in* the hospital," Nanea said. "She could be on the lawn, and the men could go outside to see her."

Lieutenant Gregory's mouth opened and then closed. He lifted a finger and then put it down. He shook his head. "You've got this all worked out, haven't you?"

"Almost." Nanea paused. "Would you talk to the

hospitals? They won't listen to a kid like me."

Lieutenant Gregory raised one eyebrow, and then he burst out laughing. "I'm sure glad you're on our side," he said. "Otherwise, we wouldn't have a chance in the world of winning this war." He stuck his hand out to shake Nanea's. "You've got a deal, Miss Mitchell."

Victory!

✺ CHAPTER 15 ✺

anea!" Mary Lou shook her. "Wake up!"

Nanea bolted out of bed. "Did the attack come?" she asked, her heart racing. She grabbed her evacuation kit, Mele's evacuation kit, and Mele.

"Come on!" Mary Lou called as she hurried out of the room.

With Mele and the evacuation kits in her arms, Nanea followed her sister to the living room. Their parents were gathered around the Philco radio. Nanea dropped the kits and sat on the floor next to Mom, Mele on her lap.

"Aloha, fellow Americans on this fine day, June sixth, 1942. This is Owen Cunningham with Captain Buckner, an eyewitness to the battle. Captain Buckner, will you set the stage for us?"

Another voice began speaking. *"Yes. As the enemy approached, we saw our fighters begin to engage them. Several went down in flames. Our heavy ground fire was too hot for them. All in all, the attack lasted about one half hour."*

"Finally, some good news!" Mom patted her chest, exhaling loudly.

"We can all take a deep breath," Papa said. "Hawaii

doesn't have to worry about more attacks."

Nanea was confused. "What does this mean?"

"We won!" Mary Lou got up and jitterbugged around the room. "We won the Battle of Midway!"

"This calls for pancakes!" Mom said, heading to the kitchen. Mary Lou followed to help her.

Nanea kept her arms around Mele. A million questions bounced around her brain. *Did this mean the end of blackouts? Of curfews? Would things finally go back to normal?* But then she realized something wonderful: *If the battle was over, David wouldn't need to join the Army! Everything was going to be all right!*

At breakfast, Nanea poured syrup over a second stack of pancakes.

Mom laughed. "You have a good appetite today!"

"The war is over!" Nanea cried, picking up her fork.

Papa set down his coffee cup. "Well, Sunshine, this is a victory. But the war isn't over."

"But Mary Lou said we won." Nanea felt like she'd been splashed in the face with icy water.

Papa nodded. "Yes. We won a very important battle. It's the first time the Japanese Navy has been stopped in the Pacific. Now our Navy has the advantage instead of theirs."

"I don't understand," Nanea said, putting her fork down. Before she could ask any more questions, David came in the back door. Everyone turned to look at him.

"Have you heard?" Nanea asked.

David nodded. "Victory at Midway! It's great news."

"Great news for us," Nanea said.

"Why is that?" David asked.

"Because now you won't have to go in the Army!"

David cleared his throat. "You know nothing can break the ties of this 'ohana, right? Nothing. Not even if one of us goes far away."

A cold feeling crept over Nanea.

"Mom, Pop." David stood tall. "You're looking at the newest member of the United States Army."

"No!" Nanea screamed.

Mom put her arms around Nanea.

"So you've enlisted," Papa said.

"Pop, I've known all along I would enlist. This business in Midway just sealed the deal." David pulled a chair up to the table. "We need fresh recruits if we're going to win the war. I can't stand by, watching from the sidelines anymore."

"Did Lieutenant Gregory talk you into this?" Mom asked.

"No," David answered. "It's my decision. All the way." He rested his arm on Mom's shoulder. "I waited until after my birthday because you all were working so hard to make it special. But this is something I need to do."

The room was so quiet that Nanea could hear the second hand ticking on the kitchen clock.

"Well, then." Papa stood. He clapped David on the shoulder. "We're proud of you, son."

Mom wiped her eyes. "When do you leave?" she asked.

"I ship out in three weeks," David answered.

Nanea pushed her plate away. "I hate the Army," she said under her breath. Then she started to cry.

"Hey, look at it this way," David said gently. "You and Mary Lou won't have to share a bedroom anymore. You can each have your own."

"I like sharing a bedroom." Nanea wiped her damp cheeks. She knew David was trying to make her feel better. But she was so sad. And mad. Mad enough that she didn't even want to talk to David. Maybe not ever again.

"It'll be okay," David said. "*I'll* be okay." He knocked on his head. "Hard as a coconut shell." He flexed his biceps. "And strong as a shark."

Nanea stood up. "I'm going for a walk," she announced.

Both her bad mood and Mele followed her out the door and down the street. She didn't realize where she was going until she found herself at her grandparents'. Instead of going inside, she marched around the house to the back garden where Tutu grew flowers for her dancers' leis. Nanea began to jerk weeds out of the ground, one after another, growing angrier by the minute. She threw the weeds this way and that. Finally, all the mad inside bubbled over and spilled out of her.

"I hate him!" she yelled, tears rolling down her cheeks. She didn't care what Mom said. She had never been so mad at her brother in her whole life. It just wasn't fair. Their family was doing so much for the war effort. Papa worked extra shifts. Mom taught first aid. Mary Lou cooked and served meals. Nanea thought about how she'd performed at USO shows and worked hard to help her class earn the Minuteman flag. Then there were all the things the

Honolulu Helpers had done for Uncle Sam—not to mention her plans for Operation Mele Medicine. Why wasn't any of that enough?

"Nanea?" Tutu stood there, looking concerned.

Nanea ducked her head so Tutu wouldn't see that she was crying. "I thought I could do some weeding for you," she said.

"Oh?" Tutu took in the weeds all over the yard. "I see. How about if we get a bucket and pick those up?"

As they worked in silence, the rhythm of tossing the weeds in the bucket calmed Nanea down a bit.

"Much better," Tutu said when they had finished. "Come sit." She motioned Nanea to follow her to the lanai.

Nanea told Tutu the news.

"Oh, keiki." Tutu patted her ample lap, and Nanea crawled into it. "I didn't know." She held Nanea close. "Our hearts can cry together."

They sat for some time, Nanea breathing in Tutu's familiar smells of coconut and coffee. After a while, Tutu Kane joined them, and Tutu quietly told him about David.

"The war has brought many changes, but this

is the biggest change of all," Tutu Kane said with a sigh. He looked at Nanea. "You know I gave your brother his Hawaiian name, right?"

Nanea nodded.

"It is a big responsibility, bestowing a name. But the minute I saw David, I was reminded of my own grandfather. David had his eyes, his nose, his determined mouth. And there wasn't a braver man than Kekoa Pono." Tutu Kane shook his head.

"David is brave," Nanea said. "He tackles waves that make other surfers stay on the beach."

"And you know the most important part of bravery?" Tutu asked.

"Strong muscles?" Nanea asked.

Tutu smiled. "Well, one strong muscle." She patted her chest. "David has a brave heart. Like you, I wish he could have made another decision. But I know he is doing what he thinks is right for his 'ohana and his country. That is true courage."

Nanea wiped at her wet face again. "I don't want David to get hurt," she whispered. It scared her to say those words.

Tutu Kane shook his head. "You have had to grow up too fast because of this war."

Nanea touched her shell necklace. That was what Tutu

Kane had said when he'd given it to her.

"Aloha," Tutu said. "Love is what carries us through times like these."

The three of them sat together in the warm sun, listening to a pair of zebra doves making their rapid-fire calls from the mango tree. Nanea took a shaky breath, filling her lungs with the sweet scents of the ginger and the tuberoses and the carnations.

"Tutu? May I ask a favor?"

"Anything," Tutu answered.

Nanea pointed to the flower garden. "May I cut some of those when David leaves? I want to make him a lei."

Good-byes and Good Deeds

Three weeks passed quickly, and then it was time for David to leave for boot camp in Mississippi. Nanea wasn't able to keep back the tears when she presented David with the lei she'd made. "Promise to throw it overboard," she demanded.

"I will, Monkey." He ruffled her hair. "But I don't need to. You can bet your bottom dollar that I'll be coming back."

Nanea's weren't the only tears as the 'ohana said their good-byes. Even Papa's eyes glistened as they waited at the fence by the dock while David marched up the steps to the pier with the other recruits.

Nanea waved to David until he was smaller than one of the shells on her necklace. And she kept waving as the boat steamed out of sight.

"We'd better get going," Papa said. "You have an important job."

"Are you sure you're up for this today?" Mom asked.

Nanea nodded. "It'll be good to have something to take my mind off David's leaving."

Shortly after they got back home, Dixie and Lily arrived. "We're here to help," Dixie said.

"I'll fill the washtub," offered Lily.

"I'll get Mele," said Nanea.

"What should I do?" asked Dixie.

"Be ready with the hose!" Nanea called.

Together, the three girls scrubbed Mele from nose to tail. They rubbed her dry with towels, fluffing up her fur.

"She looks great," Dixie said.

"But we look like drowned rats!" Lily tugged at her soaking-wet blouse. "I'm running home to change."

"Me, too! Back in a jiff." Dixie ran off to her new home at the Hills' house.

Soon they were back, and all three girls were dry and spiffed up. Nanea held tight to her 'eke hula.

"Are you ready?" Papa asked.

"Yes," Nanea nodded.

"Me, too," Dixie said, holding Mary Lou's record player in her arms.

"Not quite." Lily set down the records she was hold ing and pulled a hair ribbon from her pocket. She tied it around Mele's neck. "Now we're ready."

Lieutenant Gregory greeted them at the hospital. "The men are waiting for you in the day room," he said.

A few moments later, a no-nonsense nurse stopped

them in the hall. "Where are you going?" she asked in a voice as starched as her white hat.

"Um . . ." Nanea hesitated.

"Is there a problem, nurse?" Lieutenant Gregory asked.

"No dogs allowed." The nurse sniffed as if Mele had rolled in dead fish. "And no children either," she said.

Lieutenant Gregory looked left. He looked right. "Dog?" He scratched his head. "All I see is a four-legged hula dancer," he said.

The nurse frowned. Then she shook her head. "Hula dancer, indeed. I hope you have permission." She put her hands on her hips.

Lieutenant Gregory pulled a piece of paper out of his pocket. "We do."

The nurse scanned it. "What is this world coming to?" she grumbled. But she waved them on.

"*Mahalo,*" Nanea said. She wasn't sure the nurse heard her.

"There it is." Lieutenant Gregory nodded at a door at the far end of the hall.

Nanea paused. She thought about how she hadn't liked Lieutenant Gregory at first. Who would have thought he would have worked so hard to help put Operation Mele Medicine into place? He had pulled a lot of strings and gotten them into a room inside the hospital.

Mele tugged at her leash, looking at Nanea as if she was saying, *Well, what are we waiting for?*

"There's a room over there where you can change," Lieutenant Gregory said.

Nanea quickly put on her dance costume and then she tied Mele's on. Lily adjusted Nanea's *lei po'o*. Dixie fluffed her skirt.

"Ready?" Lily asked.

Nanea took a deep breath. She thought of David, her brave brother. With another deep breath, she straightened her shoulders and stepped into the day room. It was full of wounded men who needed some Mele medicine.

When Dixie put on the first record, Mele wagged her tail. Nanea knew the two of them had an important story to tell. A story of aloha. A story of healing.

She lifted her hands to her heart. "Let's dance, Hula Dog!"

And they did.

INSIDE
Nanea's World

Even after the Battle of Midway, people in Hawaii still saw daily reminders of the war.

The Battle of Midway was not the end of World War Two, but it was an important turning point—especially for the people of Hawaii. American forces defeated the Japanese Navy at Midway Island. Much of the tension and fear that Nanea and her neighbors had been feeling was lifted, because Hawaii was no longer on constant alert for enemy attacks.

Life, however, was not back to normal. The rules of martial law, such as curfews and blackouts, still applied. Shops, restaurants, movie theaters, and parks closed early. The worries of war still hung over the islands. People did all they could to help, but many were frustrated that they

Honolulu was crowded with soldiers, sailors, and war workers. There were long lines and lots of waiting.

The Japanese American owner of this grocery store in California put up a large sign the day after Pearl Harbor was attacked.

couldn't do more. This was especially true for Americans of Japanese ancestry. Many of them were eager to defend their country and tried enlisting in the military. Young men like Gene were told they could not serve. They were considered "enemy alien."

Although Nanea's story is fictional, the group that Gene organizes—the Varsity Victory Volunteers—was a real group formed by college students. They built roads, dug ammunition pits, and hauled stones. Their tireless work was testament to their loyalty to America. In 1943, the military allowed Japanese Americans to enlist. President Roosevelt fully supported the change, writing, "Americanism is a matter of the mind and heart; Americanism is not, and never was, a matter of race or ancestry." The Army hoped for 1,500 volunteers from Hawaii. They were stunned when nearly 10,000 Americans of Japanese ancestry signed up.

Japanese American men of all ages signed up to fight for their country.

Children all across America helped pack food boxes (above) and roll bandages (right).

Younger students were also committed to helping. Many joined church groups or clubs, like the Junior Red Cross, to roll bandages, make food packages, or knit sweaters and socks for soldiers. Girls like Nanea started their own clubs and spent their free time collecting supplies, working in Victory Gardens, volunteering in hospitals, and doing whatever they could to help in the community.

One unique way people all over the country helped was by loaning their dogs to the military. When World War Two began, the military didn't think dogs could be useful to the war effort. A group of dog trainers and breeders thought differently. They knew that dogs could be trained to do tasks such as patrolling, delivering messages, and sniffing out mines. Less than a month after the attack on Pearl Harbor, a civilian group organized Dogs for Defense and asked Americans to send their pets into service.

Certain breeds, or mixes of breeds, were accepted into the program, including Labrador retrievers, collies, boxers,

Dogs from Hawaii attended a training camp near Honolulu.

and German shepherds. The dogs went to one of five centers across the country for eight to twelve weeks of training. During that time, they were assigned a human "handler" who taught them basic voice and hand commands. Dogs also learned to get used to gunfire, riding in vehicles, and even wearing a gas mask. More than 10,000 dogs were trained and used in the Army and the Coast Guard.

Nanea couldn't imagine giving up her beloved dog. She was not alone. Many people were not willing to part with their four-legged family members. But there was still a way for those pet owners to sign their dogs up for service. For

When the war ended, military dogs went through another training—this time to help them readjust to life as pets.

one dollar they could enroll their pets in the canine Home Guard. The money that was raised helped cover the cost of the Dogs for Defense program.

Another way the government raised money was through issuing War Savings Stamps. These stamps weren't used for mailing letters. They were a way to lend money to the government, which used the funds to buy war equipment. Kids bought ten-cent stamps at school. Each stamp was placed in a special booklet that the whole class shared. When the booklet was full, the class bought a War Bond for $18.75. Kids used their allowances or the money they earned from weekend jobs to buy War Stamps and "Back the Attack."

Some students went without milk at lunch and used that money to buy War Stamps.

The people of Hawaii did more than their part when it came to buying War Stamps. There were more War Bonds purchased in Hawaii than anywhere else in the country. The government set sales goals, and islanders went above and beyond those goals all four years of the war.